"Grace is free~~d~~ interested in ~~finding work.~~

Grace's wide eyes met Peter's equally startled ones. It was difficult to determine whose jaw sagged farther.

"So, what time do you want Grace at the house tomorrow?"

Rubbing a hand over his mouth, Peter contemplated the trio of women.

"I'm out in the barn by five in the morning."

Grace's eyes widened. "Five? How did that work with Lydia watching the *kinner*?"

"The girls slept in the buggy and then at her house after I delivered them. But since you have your own buggy..." Peter's eyes challenged her. Grace read in their blue glint that he was expecting her to back out.

She would have, if her *mamm*'s summons hadn't been lying on her counter. Squaring her shoulders, Grace smiled, though it was a twitchy one. "Looks like I'll be enjoying some sunrises."

Peter's brow disappeared under his bangs. "I guess I'll see you tomorrow, then."

Publishers Weekly bestselling author **Jocelyn McClay** grew up on an Iowa farm, ultimately pursuing a degree in agriculture. She met her husband while weight lifting in a small town—he "spotted" her. After thirty years in business management, they moved to an acreage in southeastern Missouri to be closer to family when their oldest of three daughters made them grandparents. When not writing, she keeps busy grandparenting, hiking, biking, gardening, quilting, knitting and substitute teaching.

Books by Jocelyn McClay

Love Inspired

Visit the Author Profile page at LoveInspired.com for more titles.

THEIR IMPOSSIBLE AMISH MATCH

JOCELYN McCLAY

LOVE INSPIRED
INSPIRATIONAL ROMANCE

LOVE INSPIRED®
INSPIRATIONAL ROMANCE

PLEASE RECYCLE
THIS PRODUCT IS RECYCLABLE

Recycling programs
for this product may
not exist in your area.

ISBN-13: 978-1-335-93182-5

Their Impossible Amish Match

Love Inspired
22 Adelaide St. West, 41st Floor
Toronto, Ontario M5H 4E3, Canada
www.LoveInspired.com

Printed in U.S.A.

This is the day which the Lord hath made;
we will rejoice and be glad in it.
—*Psalms* 118:24

First, I thank God for this opportunity.
Thanks to Audra, for her insight into the characters.
Luke, for his willingness to answer what-if
questions at soccer games; the Bunco ladies for
their particular knowledge; Kevin for his constant
patience; and Genna, love those Wednesday calls.

Chapter One

He was married, yet he had no wife.

Or at least, not one that wanted him. Or their daughters. Or even their lifestyle. Peter Lehman's troubled gaze softened when it rested on Malinda and Fannie—still surprisingly neat in their Sunday dresses and aprons—where they were tucked in on either side of their aunt Lydia on the opposing benches that lined the center of the clean-swept barn. Though he worried about his little girls, they were his greatest joy.

Tipping his head back, Peter drew in a deep breath. His lips curved at the scent of hay from the overhead lofts and the subtle aroma of the four-legged residents that normally inhabited the cavernous building. In appreciation of the pleasant May weather after a cold Wisconsin winter, all available openings—including the big hay door near the rafters where a few curious pigeons fluttered—had been thrown open. He wasn't surprised this Sunday's hosts had decided to use the big barn for church. He would have as well.

But then, he'd always felt more comfortable in a barn than a house. Even before he'd married Lucetta. A feeling she'd exacerbated as soon as they'd said their vows, his with earnest sincerity, hers with…anything but.

Peter twisted his lips. Newly arrived in the area, he'd been a gullible fool to Lucetta's calculated lures. Their marriage had been prompted by now five-year-old Malinda's arrival and had soured immediately. But he'd made vows, and he would keep them. Two years later, Lucetta had whined that another child was on the way. Seeing his delight, she'd waspishly added that in all likelihood, it wasn't his. Peter had wiped any hint of emotion from his face and kept it that way. He'd tried to remain detached when Fannie arrived, knowing those sweet, immature features might never grow into something resembling him. But when Lucetta had thrust the red squalling infant into his arms as soon as the midwife had left, Peter had realized he didn't care who'd sired the child. She needed him, so she was his. Though Lucetta had kept the girls clothed and fed, any other maternal instincts appeared beyond her. He'd watched her treatment of the girls with consternation, but anytime he'd spoken up, it had just aggravated the situation. Though Lucetta's actions were an abomination in their Amish community, for the girls' sake, it was almost a blessing that she'd left.

In these months since her departure, he had received some surprising but much-needed assistance from her sister Lydia, who, in addition to her own yearling son, had taken care of his girls while he strived to make a go of the farm his uncle had left him.

Nee, Fannie's biological parentage didn't matter—he was her father. Though her situation had, at the time, prompted him to even wonder about his older daughter, Lucetta had assured him Malinda was his child. Probably because he'd been the one fool enough to marry her. Peter shifted his attention to his older daughter and stiffened when the little girl's eyes widened. Following her lifted gaze, he saw Lydia, her eyes closed, tipping in Malinda's direction.

He was about to jab his seatmate Jonah, Lydia's husband, when a young woman sitting behind the trio on the backless benches reached out to grasp his sister-in-law's tilting shoulder. Lydia jerked upright, her eyes blinking furiously, her face flushing enough to challenge the red in her hair.

Peter stifled a smile. Lydia wouldn't be the first to fall asleep during the long church service. Any urge toward amusement faded, though, when Lydia lightly pressed a hand to her stomach.

A private smile touched her lips as she glanced over at his friend, who was currently bouncing their young son on his lap. Peter darted a look at Jonah. He had the answer to his unspoken question when the man's cheeks reddened above the newly grown beard that all married men sported.

Sighing quietly so the obviously proud father-to-be beside him wouldn't notice, Peter gritted his teeth. He was happy for the couple. Truly he was. Jonah and Lydia had endured a rough start to their relationship and parenthood. They deserved their happiness.

But it left him in a bind.

Although he might selfishly want to, he could not in good conscience expect Lydia to watch his two young daughters. Not when he now noticed, by her hollowed cheeks and the smudges under her eyes, that the pending arrival, along with the care of three little ones, was taking a toll on her. Not when she'd done so much for him already.

Feeling a little ill, he was tempted to press a hand against his own stomach. If not Lydia, who could watch his girls? When his fields were buried under snow and he worked close to the house and barn, he'd kept them with him. Now, with planting and other fieldwork needing to be done, he couldn't keep the girls and work. Farming was too dangerous.

For a nauseating moment, he considered selling the farm he'd inherited and returning to Kentucky. At least there he had some family to help with the girls. But doing so would be giving up his dream of his own place to go back to working for someone else. He wasn't ready to give up. Not yet, at least. But the girls came first. If there was no other help for them...

With compressed lips, he scanned the opposing benches of women and girls. Several were married, some with businesses and others with several small children of their own already. Though they might be willing to take on his girls, he was reluctant to ask. He couldn't afford to pay much, and he hated being a burden to anyone. With Lucetta's behavior, he already felt like a fool in the community.

His gaze flicked back to the rows behind the married women, where the single and younger girls sat. Perhaps one of them would be interested in watching Malinda and Fannie now that school was out for the summer. Most of the older ones already had jobs. His gaze lingered on the blonde who'd prevented Lydia from tipping. His gaze and probably every single man's over the age of thirteen. The younger males had likely seen the woman frequently enough in the classroom over the past school year. Peter lifted an eyebrow. How many of those boys had developed a crush on their pretty teacher? His lips twitched.

He might've if he were that age. Back when he'd had the confidence to do so. Back when he'd had more trust in pretty women. *Nee*, she wouldn't do at all.

He forced his gaze to move on. At least, as a married man, no one he hired would be foolish enough to indulge an interest in him. Even if he was single, between his girls and the farm, he had no energy for that. And no interest either. He scowled. Lucetta had made sure of that. Would she make sure by leaving that he had to give up the farm as well? With a hard swallow, Peter folded his arms across his chest. He had to find someone to help with his girls.

Grace Kauffman kept her expression composed as she dropped her gaze to her lap. Hopefully no one in the airy barn would realize her mind was far from the second sermon of the day. Her thoughts instead were focused on the letter on her kitchen counter, the one from her *mamm*.

The letter asking her to come home to Iowa.

Grace grimaced. She taught the niceties of letter writing to her students. Even the ones still laboriously printing in block letters would've recognized the nuance. Her mother's missive wasn't *asking* her to come home. It was *telling* her to.

Her shoulders sagged. She had a tendency, *nee*, more of a habit, to do as others' wished. She liked to please people. To make them happy. Normally she would've reluctantly packed up and done as her *mamm* requested. But the reason her mother demanded her presence was the same one that had Grace dragging her feet like she was sloughing through hip-deep Wisconsin snow.

Willis was available again.

Grace tightened her fist around the fabric of her apron before immediately releasing it to smooth out any wrinkles. Willis hadn't wanted her the first time around. Her *mamm* and his, best friends from childhood, had pushed the pair of them together so fiercely that Grace was surprised there weren't skid marks on the road between the two farms. Skid marks at least from the direction of Willis's place. She had let herself be persuaded. Had even convinced herself she was in love with him. Except for one little detail. He hadn't returned her interest. Not really. Not at all.

Grace had been mortified at how Willis had revealed that little detail.

Thankfully, *Gott* had answered her prayers and provided this job teaching in Miller's Creek. She'd hurriedly packed under her *mamm*'s disgruntled gaze, left the week before Willis and Cora's wedding, and had never returned. In the time since, she'd grown to love her adopted community and the friends she'd made here.

She had plunked into a nearby chair when she'd

read in the letter that Cora had been kicked in the head by a horse. But regardless of her *mamm*'s expectations, just because Willis was a young widower, it was doubtful he'd be any more interested in Grace now than he had been earlier. There was no use, though, in telling two determined matchmaking mothers that. Grace knew them. They hadn't listened before. Now would be no different.

If she went home, she would eventually, reluctantly, succumb to their plans. Again. With the same humiliating results, because she also knew Willis.

So her best protection, her best defense, was to maintain a safe distance. To stay the two hundred plus miles away in Wisconsin. Though, now that school in Miller's Creek was out for the summer, she no longer had a reason to.

Her *mamm* wasn't of a patient nature. A return letter to her would soon need to be in the mail. Grace sighed. But what would it say? How would she refuse her *mamm* when she normally…didn't? Grace lifted her head as the minister wrapped up his sermon. At least he hadn't spoken today on honoring thy father and mother.

She joined in the final hymns, but even the normally comforting slow songs weren't enough to distract her. Which is why, when the service finally ended, she was glad to push up from the backless benches and tap her friend Lydia on the shoulder.

"I didn't mean to startle you, but you kept tipping and tipping and I was concerned you were going to tumble right over. Are you all right?"

Lydia looked up from where she was helping the younger of two little girls down from the bench. "*Denki.* I was glad of your rescue. Otherwise I might've used Malinda here as an unintended cushion. And, *ja,* I'm fine. Just a little tired lately."

"Anything I can do? I'd be happy to help." Grace smiled ruefully. "Particularly if doing so would give me a reason to stay in Miller's Creek over the summer."

Lydia frowned. "Why wouldn't you stay?"

Grace drew in a relieved breath at the prompt support. When Lydia had first returned to the district last fall, Grace had been apprehensive about the young woman due to her reputation. Apprehension had turned into a fast friendship when Lydia had defended her in the face of a damaging rumor, one started by Lydia's own sister.

"Of course you'll stay over the summer. You did last year, *ja*?" A young woman, with a toddler on her hip and a slight bump under her apron indicating its sibling was on the way, paused as she made her way between the church benches.

Grace smiled at the newcomer. Miriam Raber

had become another good friend. "My *mamm* wants me to come home."

Miriam lifted a brow. "For a *gut* reason?"

"*Gut* for her." Grace grimaced. "Not so *gut* for me."

"Just for the summer?" Miriam shifted the toddler to her other hip.

Grace blew out a long breath. "*Nee*. If she has her way, I'd be returning to Iowa for *gut*."

"Well, then. For sure and certain, we'll need to keep you here."

"I wish it were that simple. I'd need a reason she'd accept." Otherwise, Grace wouldn't be surprised if her *mamm* sent someone up to help her pack.

"A job?" Lydia suggested.

"A beau?" Miriam's second eyebrow joined the first. "Or, better yet, a job until the beau becomes a spouse? Surely your *mamm* would find that a *gut* enough reason to stay."

Grace's own smile was weak. Though the prospect was appealing to her, it was one her mother definitely wouldn't be satisfied with. Not when she intended Grace to marry her best friend's son.

Miriam apparently read her expression. "Or just whichever comes first," she added.

The trio of women looked over when Lydia's younger charge scrambled back up on the bench and lifted her arms. A dark-haired man approached and swung the girl easily into his arms before quickly adjusting her to make room to gather in her older sister as well.

"I was coming over to collect the benches to take to the house for the noon meal. What do you think they'd say if I delivered you two instead?"

Grace was surprised at the man's teasing comments. She could only recall hearing Peter Lehman saying a word or two the whole time she'd been in the district.

"That you're silly, *Daed.*" The younger girl patted his cheek.

"Only for you two." The man's smiling gaze immediately sobered when, after a quick glance that encompassed Grace and Miriam, he focused his attention on Lydia. What he saw must have bothered him, because the strong column of his throat bobbed as he swallowed.

"When you have a moment later today, I'd like to talk with you." His voice was as grave as his expression.

"She has a moment now, Peter." When Miriam's comment was rewarded with the young man's scowl, she grinned, undeterred. "Oh. You mean a moment without company."

"It's all right, Peter. What do you need?"

Peter's wary glance again darted between Grace and Miriam. Under his worn collarless *mutza* jacket, his broad chest rose on a deep sigh.

"I need to know if they're—" he tipped his head toward the girls in his arms "—too much for you. Especially since…" He cleared his throat.

Grace's eyebrows rose when the man's ears reddened.

"Well, since—" He glanced at Lydia's midsection meaningfully.

"Oh." Lydia blushed as she touched her apron. "I actually think the worst—" She broke off to cast a puzzled glance in Miriam's direction.

Glancing down, Grace saw the blond woman's toe gently tapping Lydia's black shoe. She lifted her gaze to catch Miriam pointedly looking in her direction.

Lydia's lips twitched. "Um… I actually think the worst may be yet to come. I love having the girls. They're dears. But a…" her gaze darted between a smirking Miriam and Grace "…a small break would be helpful?" Her voice lifted at the end, like it was a question.

When Peter winced, Grace felt sorry for the man. Though she only knew him as Lydia's brother-in-law, she, like everyone else in the district, knew of his situation regarding his absent wife. Why would Miriam be teasing him so?

The man drew in a long breath, but before he could speak, Miriam piped in. "Grace was just mentioning that since school is out, she's free for the summer and is interested in finding work.

Seems like there's an easy solution to the situation. Looks like it's a *gut* thing we joined your conversation after all, Peter."

Grace's wide eyes met Peter's equally startled ones. It was difficult to determine whose jaw sagged farther before his immediately snapped shut with a *click*.

Chapter Two

Grace's jaw closed in time for a hard swallow when Peter's gaze narrowed on her. "I can't pay much."

"That's all right. She doesn't need much. The school district already provides her with lodging and a horse and buggy as part of her wages. She's *wunderbar* with children."

Grace winced. Miriam sounded like an auctioneer trying to encourage reluctant bidders, with Grace as the item on the block. Meanwhile, the potential buyer looked like he wished he'd never come to the sale.

"And she can start this week. Which is *gut* because Lydia does look…" Miriam arched a glance in the other woman's direction "…incredibly tired."

Lydia's brow furrowed a moment before she abruptly raised a hand to her mouth to cover an exaggerated yawn. Grace, stifling a giggle, had to look away.

"So, what time do you want Grace at the house tomorrow?"

Grace could now understand how forthright Miriam had won the heart of a reformed Aaron Raber when he'd returned to the community after time spent with the *Englisch*. And how she'd easily handled her three older brothers prior to her marriage.

Peter carefully set his girls down to stand on the bench, the only one remaining in the cavernous barn. All others had been carried out when the rest of the men, sending curious glances in their direction, had exited. Rubbing a hand over his mouth, Peter contemplated the trio of women on the far side of the plank.

"I'm out in the barn by five in the morning."

Grace's eyes widened at the early hour. He sent her a humorless smile.

She was used to rising early. Or what she'd thought was early. "Five? How did that work with Lydia watching the *kinner*?"

"The girls slept in the buggy and then at her house after I delivered them. But since you have your own buggy…" Peter's eyes challenged her. Grace read in their blue glint that he was expecting her to back out. And would be happy when she did.

She would have, if her *mamm*'s summons hadn't been lying on her counter. Squaring her shoulders, Grace smiled, though it was a twitchy one. "Looks like I'll be enjoying some sunrises."

"I guess I'll see you tomorrow, then," he acknowledged before his lips became as flat as the bench between them.

"I guess you will." Grace strove not to drop her gaze under his penetrating one. *Begin as you mean to go on.* If she shied away from his obvious displeasure now, what would she do when she didn't have her two friends behind her for support? *I can do this. I manage fourteen-year-old boys who'd rather be fishing than adding or subtracting on a chalkboard. I can handle one father who, for some reason, doesn't like me. Especially if once he goes to the barn in the morning, he stays there a while.* Grace's eyes finally slid from Peter's intense gaze to the knot in his clenched jaw. *A long while. Because he wouldn't need help with his girls if he were constantly around. Would he?*

"Well—" Grace flinched at the muted *smack* when Lydia clasped her hands together, drawing everyone's attention "—I look forward to spending time with the girls today since they won't be coming to my house this week. Malinda and Fannie, let's go see if they have a church spread inside. I know it's one of your favorites." Casting a pointed glance in Grace's direction, Lydia paused. "And if they don't have sandwiches already made, perhaps Grace here can help you make one."

Grace appreciated Lydia giving her a chance to get to know her new charges. Better now than when they woke up tomorrow morning to find her in their house. With a smile, she offered a hand to each girl. They gave her a wary glance. Grace snorted softly. *Ja*, they certainly took after their father. But to her surprise, when the girls shot a look in his direction, after a brief pause, their *daed* gave them an abrupt nod. Even so, ignoring her outstretched hands, the girls scrambled from the bench by themselves. Once on the ground, they tucked their hands behind their backs.

With a concerned frown, Peter bent to briefly cup each of their cheeks in a gentle palm, a silent message in his blue eyes. When he straightened, he hefted the now empty bench with an easy jerk and exited out the barn door.

When his broad back disappeared from view, Grace rolled her eyes at her friends. "I can't believe you pestered the poor man like that. What were you doing?"

Miriam's expression was pensive as she stared at the recently vacated barn door. "Peter needs some…joy. Aaron got to know him when Peter first moved into the area. Aaron said he was different then. Happier. Hopeful. At least until Lucetta got ahold of him." She clasped a hand over her mouth as her gaze ricocheted from Lydia to the little girls and back again.

"No offense taken here. I'm disappointed in my sister myself," Lydia assured her.

"Still, I shouldn't have said it. But since I did, I suppose I feel sorry for him. He works so hard. And—" her gaze rested on the two girls as her voice lowered "—*happy* and *hopeful* aren't words I'd use to describe the situation your sister left him in. Besides, you wanted a reason to stay." She grinned. "Now you've got one."

Grace smiled wryly. "Thank you. I think. A reason who looks like he can't stand the sight of me. But two—" she squatted until she was the same level as her future charges "—who look delightful. Hello." She addressed the girls. "My name is Grace. I'm a friend of your aunt Lydia. I think I've heard your names mentioned. Let's see if I can remember and guess who's who. Hmm." She tapped her finger on her cheek in feigned concentration before tipping her head toward the younger girl. "Are you… Cinnamon and your older sister Ginger?" She voiced the names chalked on the horse stalls behind the girls. "Or is it the other way around?"

The two sisters looked at each other, their lips twitching toward smiles before they schooled themselves to bland expressions. A shard of pain speared Grace at the caution in such little ones.

The older one turned back to Grace and, after a brief hesitation, touched herself on the chest. "*Nee.* I'm Malinda and that's—" she pointed to her sister "—Fannie."

"Oh, those are nice names. So nice that I want to make sure I don't forget and call you Cinnamon and Ginger again tomorrow morning when you come down to breakfast. Maybe I should practice." She stood and offered her hands again. "Would you, Malinda, and you, Fannie, come with me into the kitchen? I'm hoping that along with a church spread sandwich, we can also find a whoopie pie or two. It's one of my favorites."

The younger girl's fist crept from behind her back. It hovered a moment by her side before she lifted it to wrap miniature fingers around Grace's outstretched hand. Grace smiled, her chest expanding as unexpected relief filled her. She worked with shy children all the time. Why would the acceptance of this unanticipated one mean so much?

Malinda, the older sister, regarded Grace solemnly before extending her own hand. Though tempted, Grace didn't reach for it, instead, letting the girl cross the final distance to clasp her cool fingers. "I think Cinnamon and Ginger are better names for horses than they are for little girls.

Do you have horses at your farm?" She steered the two toward the barn's big open double doors. From the footsteps that echoed through the now empty space, she knew Lydia and Miriam were following close behind.

"Hazel pulls the buggy. We have many big horses. One is named Bella. She's going to have a *boppeli*." Grace had to lean down to hear Fannie's whisper.

"It's a *foal*, not a *boppeli*. Those are for people, not horses." Malinda corrected.

"That sounds exciting. Is the foal coming soon?" Grace took the girls' willingness to converse with her as another victory. She'd seen them with their aunt before at community events but had never approached Lydia at those times.

"Not soon enough. *Daed* isn't going to use Bella for fieldwork this year. The foal is too important."

"That sounds like a wise decision."

"My *daed* is wise," Malinda asserted loyally.

"Mine too," seconded Fannie.

Grace bit her tongue. The man might be wise, but he wasn't particularly friendly. "I look forward to getting to know him," she murmured neutrally.

Miriam fell into step beside them. "Well, the job part is taken care of. Now we just need to remedy the beau situation."

"One thing at a time." Though the girls were charming, Grace was apprehensive of what her friends would come up with regarding a beau. Her *mamm*'s pressure, albeit distant, pressed heavily enough already on that front. "At least I have a job now. On the other, *ach*, we'll see what I can come up with myself."

"All right. But I'll be thinking about it for you." Miriam smooched the cheek of the toddler on her hip. "I've been so happy in wedded life, I want everyone to join in."

Lydia smiled. "And I second that."

"Where's your little one?" Grace strove to head off discussion on beaus.

"Jonah probably heard our conversation with Peter and figured it was safer just to keep his son," Miriam teased.

Lydia's husband materialized as soon as they stepped outside the big barn doors. Caleb, spying his *mamm*, leaned away from his *daed* to reach for her. Lydia's grin was as wide as her open arms as she received him. The young parents shared a private look and smile over the top of the boy's head before Jonah went to join the congregating men.

Observing the happy pair, Grace sighed. It would be nice to be part of a couple. But if she returned to Iowa and the widowed Willis, *happy* might not be an apt description of her future relationship. Not with what had happened before. Nor with unyielding parental pressure as the primary reason for their union.

Now, thanks to her friends, she didn't have to face that. Grace grinned at the two girls and was rewarded when they tentatively smiled in return. For these sweet little ones and a reason to stay in Wisconsin, she'd tolerate their unfriendly father.

"Why are we leaving so early today, *Daed*?"

Peter scowled. He didn't have a good answer to Malinda's question. He focused his attention on Hazel's twitching ears as the Standardbred trotted toward home. "I wanted to check on Bella." His stomach twisted as soon as the words left him. After living with Lucetta's continuous falsehoods, he'd vowed not to be dishonest with the girls, even for lies with few or no consequences. Still…he ran his fingers through his short beard. "Um… I just needed to get home today."

Needed to get away from the feeling that he'd been manipulated. Again.

"Why is the new *weibsmensch* coming tomorrow instead of us going to *Aendi* Lydia's house?"

It was almost as if Malinda could read his mind. But then, he knew his girls were sensitive to emotions. They'd had to be, growing up with their moody mother. Peter lifted his hand to knead the rigid tendons at the back of his neck.

"The woman is coming because Aunt Lydia can't watch you right now."

"Why not?"

"Well—" Peter's neck wasn't getting any less stiff at Malinda's persistence on things he didn't have a good explanation for "—she's extra tired right now because she is…" How did he explain his sister-in-law's condition to his daughters? His determination not to lie to his girls now mocked him.

The Amish didn't normally speak of pregnancies, particularly to children. As oldest in his family, he recalled the many times his *mamm*'s middle had swelled under her apron until one day, months later, a new sibling would arrive with no explanation. He'd like to blame the reason for his marriage to Lucetta on the lack of discussions regarding the facts of life, but, having grown up on a farm with livestock, he had no excuses.

"Is she going to die?"

Peter whipped his head around to see Fannie's quivering lip and tear-filled eyes. "Oh, *nee*, little one." Another thing learned young in farm life. Creatures don't always survive. Even with the best of care. "This is only temporary. She'll soon be all right."

"Does Caleb have to go somewhere else too?"

Peter shook his head, both to his bewilderment at how to respond to his growing girls and to Malinda's specific question.

"*Nee*. Caleb will stay with his *mamm*."

For a moment, beyond the *clip-clop* of Hazel's hooves, it was quiet in the buggy. Peter drew in a relieved breath, thinking the worst of the questions were over. He was wrong.

"Does she not want us anymore, like our *mamm* didn't?"

"Oh, *nee*, Malinda. That isn't it at all." Following a quick check for traffic, Peter jabbed the reins under his thigh, freeing up his hands to gather his daughters into his lap. They huddled against his chest as he tucked his chin against their little *kapps*. Social discretion could be thrown to the wind. His girls were more important.

"You won't stay with Aunt Lydia's for a while because she is going to have a *boppeli*. Sometimes when a *boppeli* is coming, a *mamm* gets a little extra tired and…overwhelmed." Peter blew out a breath. As does a *daed* when he is parenting on his own and doesn't have the answers to his children's questions. Or needs. Recalling Malinda's forlorn face from a moment ago, he cuddled them closer.

"Like why you're not using Bella in the fields, because of the *boppeli* she'll have soon?"

Peter's lips twitched. "Something like that.

After Aunt Lydia starts to feel better and is less tired, she'll be able to take care of you again." *I hope.* Because as much as today's unexpected outcome was an answer to an unspoken prayer, surely *Gott* could've answered it with a fourteen-year-old girl just finishing her education. Not an older one. Not one who was a bit…pert. And more than a bit…attractive.

Like his wife had been when he'd first met her.

Alluring features he'd responded to before learning that, as the saying went, beauty was only skin deep. Peter retrieved the reins from beneath his thigh and handed one line to each girl. Hazel knew the way home anyway.

Malinda held her line lightly, just the way he'd taught her. "That's *gut.* 'Cause Grace may not stay long. She just wants a job till she can find a beau and get married. At least that's what Miriam said."

"Oh, she does, does she?" Peter abruptly stiffened. Good thing the girls held the reins; otherwise, Hazel would've been in for a rude surprise. His lips twisted. The situation might suit this woman even less than it did him. She was on the hunt for a beau? Working at his house was a dead end on that pursuit. He'd already been tricked into marriage.

"I hope she doesn't find one soon," Fannie piped up. "'Cause I like her."

Peter's chest, inflating with righteous indignation for any unsuspecting single man in the district, immediately deflated. If the girls liked this Grace, he'd have to tolerate her. At least for a while. He scowled as he tried to recall how long the tired and nauseous phase of pregnancy lasted. His shoulders sagged. Some women were sick the full nine months. He certainly hoped that wasn't the case with Lydia. But he might have to put up with this… Grace woman for a while. Maybe even until school started and she went back to her teaching job.

Well, the name certainly fit her. Lithe form, blond hair the color of sunshine on an oat field just before harvest and blue eyes like those of the baby kittens the girls frequently found in the barn. He and every other man had noticed her when she'd moved into the area a few years ago. Peter grimaced. He'd looked. Momentarily. He had eyes, didn't he? But that was all he'd done.

He'd already been tied to Lucetta. For life. With her up and down moods—mostly down— and then the gut-wrenching discovery that once their vows were spoken, she didn't want him anymore. Bile rose in the back of his throat. Peter swallowed it down, practiced at doing so regarding his wife.

He'd punished his foolishness for getting trapped by simply listening as Lucetta slipped away at night. He'd stare at the dark ceiling in the *daadi haus*'s spartan bedroom, anguishing over what to do about it. If he'd said something, Lucetta would have found some way to take it out on the girls, knowing that was the best way to hurt him. She wouldn't hurt them physically, but not all wounds were visible. So he'd said nothing, feeling less than a man in his own home for not confronting his wandering wife. And now, she'd wandered totally out of their lives. At least physically. Peter drew in a breath, shutting his eyes briefly as he strove to close his mind to painful memories.

Unfortunately, when that door closed, what popped into an open window was the new *weibsmensch*, as Malinda had called her. It was a surprise, with as many men as had been looking, that this Grace wasn't married yet. Particularly if she was looking herself. Maybe something was wrong with her. Whatever it was, it wasn't evident on the outside.

But it had to be something. If she was going to be in his house all day with the girls, he'd suss it out. Find out what was really beneath the pretty package. And warn others. *Like others had tried to warn me about Lucetta.* Peter grimaced. Unfortunately, a man enamored by a woman sometimes didn't listen to others' advice. By then, it had been too late. For him, anyway. He'd been trapped.

Peter gently guided the girls' small hands as they directed Hazel into the lane. *Ach*, what was done was done. He'd agreed to today's arrangement. What was the worst that could happen to him? He was already tied for the rest of his life to a woman who'd manipulated him and then despised him.

Chapter Three

A solitary light glowed from the dark silhouette of the Lehman farmhouse as Grace directed her mare up the lane. With sweaty palms, she drew the Standardbred to a halt at the hitching post just outside the yard fence. Well, she was here. A glance toward the east confirmed an orange cast just evident above the horizon. And before the decreed time.

Now what?

She stared at the house. Did she really want this job? It was too much to hope that the old farmhouse's interior glow was because the girls, and not their father, were up. Grace slid her hands down the front of her apron. She was as nervous as she had been the first day she'd taught school. And this was for care of only two little girls, not twenty or more students of various ages. Two little girls who'd charmed her yesterday after church.

But there was their father, who wouldn't know charm if it, like his suspenders, straddled his shoulders. His very broad shoulders. His broad *attractive* shoulders. Grimacing, Grace forced their image from her mind as she secured the reins and grabbed the bag on the seat beside her before climbing down from the buggy.

Those broad shoulders belonged to a married man. It didn't matter if the girls' father was attractive in appearance. Willis had been comely as well. Something she'd foolishly admired before the man had humiliated her. So her choices were this unexpected job, a possibly fruitless search for another one or going back to Iowa and facing Willis again.

Grace tied the mare to the hitching post and trudged up the walk toward the door. After a series of deep breaths, she raised her hand. And jumped when the door swung open before contact.

If the door opening unexpectedly startled her, what it revealed glued her tongue to the roof of her mouth and her feet to the front step. Peter Lehman stood in the opening, rubbing a small towel over his face and the damp ends of his hair. Beads of water glistened on his neck and upper chest in the open V of his collarless shirt. Grace peeled her tongue free and swallowed hard. It wasn't only the man's shoulders that were attractive. The rest of him was…unsettling as well. What flaws he had on the exterior were limited to the foamy dab of shaving cream just under his high cheekbone.

When her gaze wanted to linger on that spot, Grace deliberately dropped it, only to find herself staring at the hollow in the masculine column of his throat and the drops of water that hovered on sun-brown skin. Her eyes widened. *Speaking of foolishness in finding someone attractive! It doesn't matter that his wife jumped the fence to be with an* Englischer. *The man is still married.* Jerking her attention toward the dim kitchen behind him, Grace jabbed a thumb over her shoulder.

"I'm here. What do I do with my mare?"

Peter swiped his face with the towel. "I'll take care of her when I do chores."

A cautious glance revealed the dab of shaving cream had disappeared. The way he continued to unsettle her hadn't, though. The man couldn't do his chores soon enough to suit her.

"You're not on your way out now?"

His lips twisted. "You sound disappointed. I figured it'd be helpful to spend a few minutes going over any questions you might have." When her eyes flickered, he continued, his voice as rigid as the knot flexing in his jaw. "Regarding the girls."

Grace's face flamed at the insinuation she wanted to pry into his absent wife and personal life—the kind of gossip that'd already rippled like a fast-moving stream throughout the district. "Oh. Of course. You'd just mentioned yesterday that you go out at five. It's—" she glanced toward where the sun was peeking over the horizon "—past that now."

"Are you calling me dishonest or just lazy?" The charge, though quiet, came through gritted teeth.

Heat now raced up the back of Grace's neck, almost as if the rising sun was beating directly at her nape instead of stretching its fingers across the sky. She kept her eyes fixed on the growing illumination like she'd never seen such a sight before. "*Nee.* Not at all."

My, but the man was prickly. While the dab of shaving cream had disappeared with a single swipe, his personality flaws weren't as easily remedied. If he was the only option for staying in Miller's Creek, maybe a return to Iowa wouldn't be so bad after all.

Peter didn't follow Grace's gaze toward the orange glow that was growing over the fields. With her golden hair and glowing cheeks, she looked like a sunrise right in front of him. *I'm supposed to be looking for faults, not gawking at her.* He stepped back and opened the door farther. "Well, do you? Have any questions about the girls?"

"Um…" She entered the kitchen and looked around. Peter's gut twisted. He knew what she was seeing in the shadowy space. Worn linoleum. Crooked cupboard doors hanging on tarnished hinges. A stained enamel sink that would be evident when the sun made its way through grimy windows.

While he'd worked hard on the rest of the farm, the kitchen—and most of the house, for that matter—hadn't changed from when his bachelor uncle had lived here. Much to Lucetta's dissatisfaction. He'd tried to explain to her that the farm supported them while cosmetic expenditures on the house didn't. That if she was patient and gave him time to improve the one, the other would eventually follow. But his wife just claimed life with him was a drudgery and he was a disappointment. Neither patience nor hard work had been in her nature.

He'd gotten up particularly early this morning and had hustled, quietly so as not to wake the girls, to improve the state of the house. Something he'd longed to do yesterday when they'd returned home. Instead, he'd interacted with the girls, the piles and dust that he was too busy during the day and too tired after dark to address lurking like an impatient beast, while he abided by the Lord's admonishment not to work on the Sabbath.

Six days shall work be done: but the seventh day is the Sabbath of rest, a holy convocation; ye shall do no work therein: it is the Sabbath of the LORD in all your dwellings.

He had no fear of hard work. But the farm and the girls left very little time to apply it to the house. Still, he would rather take his girls somewhere else for care instead of having the schoolteacher come here and see the embarrassing state of his home.

Gut thing the phrase 'Cleanliness is next to godliness' wasn't actually in the *Biewel*. Given the condition of the house, godliness was currently so far away, he'd have to hire a driver to reach it—with the mileage there so great that he couldn't afford the trip anyway.

The sun had escaped the horizon, revealing more of the dingy room. Peter sighed. When she saw the true state of things, she'd probably leave so fast he wouldn't have to worry about putting her horse up. Well, he'd wanted her gone anyway. He'd still have the childcare problem, and it might disappoint the girls, but he'd rather face those issues than deal with another manipulative woman.

At least this one was punctual. Now he was the one who was late in heading out. And he was finding himself surprisingly reluctant to go.

"What do the girls like to eat?"

Peter flinched, jerking the towel until it dug into the back of his neck. "What?"

Grace set the bag she was carrying on the table. "You asked if I had any questions. What do the girls like to eat? And do you mind—" she gestured with an open hand toward the cupboards "—if I go through them to see what you have on hand and what shopping might be needed to fix meals?"

Peter scowled. What she'd find was a lot of convenience food. And probably a few spiders in the deeper regions. "Go ahead."

"When do they need to be fed, and…" She glanced away. Was that a grimace chasing across her face? "Will you be coming in to eat as well?"

"Noon. And probably." His stomach protested that it would happily show up, considering he'd been cleaning this morning when he usually grabbed a bit of breakfast. "The horses need a midday rest."

"What time do the girls usually get up?"

That question was answered by the padding of little feet. The two girls, their short, worn nightgowns revealing more of their legs than the garments should, peeked around the doorjamb into the kitchen.

"You came!" Fannie's face brightened with a smile as she trotted over to the schoolteacher.

After a brief hesitation, Malinda followed more slowly.

Grace knelt to their level. "Of course I did. I told you yesterday I would."

Malinda's lips twisted and she looked up at Peter with solemn eyes. His stomach clenched again, this time with regret. He knew what his daughter was thinking. In this household, words hadn't always been followed with actions. Lucetta had left the house months ago, yet her legacy of falsehoods lived on.

He lifted the towel from around his neck, looped it over Malinda's shoulders and used it to swish her back and forth, like she was in the old gas-powered washing machine that sat on the back porch. Something he'd gotten for Lucetta early in their marriage when it was obvious things weren't going well for the newlyweds. Back when he'd had hopes and dreams and assumed his wife shared them. Assumed she would be pleased by something he'd done for her. Assumed she'd be pleased with him.

How wrong he'd been.

But the smile from his older daughter was a reward in itself. Peter returned it, along with a quick scan of her and her sister. The house might not be clean, but the girls were. At least she'd find them well cared for.

At a question from Grace, Malinda turned from

him to give the schoolteacher a faint smile. Peter wanted to sag with relief at how well Grace was getting on with his girls. But suspicion hummed through him. Was she sincere? After all, Lucetta had seemed charming and pleasant. At first.

"If you two are up, for sure and certain, the ones in the barn are as well. I need to be out there feeding them." He retrieved the towel from around Malinda and fisted it in his hands. "She was wondering what you liked to eat. I told her frog's tails and turtle ears, but we were out of them. So you might have to come up with something else."

Fannie yanked on his pant leg. "Frogs don't have tails."

"*Ach*, no wonder we're out of them then." Peter gave the top of her head a gentle pat before heading toward the small bathroom where he'd been shaving when he'd heard the buggy approach. With a frown in the tiny mirror he used for the task, he folded the towel and set it on the vanity. How had things come to this point? When he'd arrived in Miller's Creek years ago, he'd been so hopeful, so excited, so…confident. Thanks to his uncle, he had a piece of land where, with hard work and determination, he could fulfill the dream of having a place of his own. He'd met a girl, fulfilling another dream—one of a devoted wife to work with him in building a family and successful farm. Or so he'd thought. But Lucetta had plans of her own. And he'd only been a brief part of them.

Peter's lips curved as he heard the murmur of childish voices. He had a family—part of one anyway—now. If he was to keep the farm he'd dreamed of, he needed to accept some help from this woman. At least until he found another option. As long as she treated the girls well, he didn't have to trust her motives. He'd lived without trusting for several years now.

He stepped back into the kitchen, ignoring Grace and giving a nod to the girls as he headed for the door. As the door clicked closed behind him, a peculiar tension ebbed from his shoulders. Peter resisted the urge to slump against the wall, albeit briefly. Tugging his hat on, he started across the farmyard.

The mare tied to the hitching post flicked her ears in his direction. Peter slowed a step before continuing toward the barn. He'd return for her after he tended his stock and prepared someplace to keep her. He snorted softly. Much easier dealing with the mare than her mistress.

As was his custom when he stepped out of the house in the morning, Peter's gaze swept over the farm, ensuring all was well. He always enjoyed watching the farm wake up for the day. The sights and sounds of the stirring animals in the outside lots. The rising sun's glow as it highlighted the verdant green of a nearby alfalfa field. He inhaled at the sight, the early morning air that filled his lungs so fresh he could almost taste it.

This is the day which the Lord hath made; we will rejoice and be glad in it.

Peter twisted his lips as the forgotten verse sprang to mind. *Well, I failed that one. I haven't rejoiced in a long time.* Reaching the large white double doors, he lifted the hook that secured them. *I used to be one for rejoicing.* His hands stilled on the solid metal. *I used to like that man. What happened to him? Is he gone for good?*

He jerked the heavy doors apart, afraid the answer was a resounding yes.

Chapter Four

A quiet symphony greeted Peter as he slipped through the opening in the double doors. The nickered hellos of the horses, the petulant moo of his solitary cow complaining of his tardiness, the rustling of the two half-grown hogs who didn't know that although he was feeding them now, they'd be feeding him throughout the winter. Their associated scents were underscored by the aroma of hay. Peter loved it all. Closing his eyes, he paused for a moment to soak it into his soul.

Lucetta had made him doubt everything. His manhood. His ability to support his family. His faith. Women. Fatherhood. Thankfully, based on the responses he received from the girls, he'd regained the last.

One thing he'd always been certain of, though, was his passion for farming and his livestock. When all things around him had been falling apart, he'd gone to the field, the barn, the pastures, to find peace.

Even now, the tension at the back of his neck was unraveling, and the cut of his suspenders eased as his shoulders relaxed. When he opened his eyes to cross to the biggest stall in the vast barn, his heart rate slowed to match the echo of his easy stride on the straw-strewn concrete floor.

"How's my girl today? Or should I say, 'my big girl'?" He stroked a gentle hand down the huge head that hung over the stall door. The Belgian mare's chestnut back was taller than the top of his head, her hooves the size of buckets. Peter smiled as her brown eyes closed in bliss at his petting. *Gut* thing she was as gentle as a hand-reared kitten, because weighing over a ton, the big horse would be uncontrollable if she were so inclined.

"Got a lot riding on you, Bella. A lot of hope in the foal you'll soon have." Financial hope. Bella had excellent bloodlines. Peter had brought her as a yearling with him when he'd moved up from Kentucky. For years, any available money he hadn't spent trying to appease Lucetta had been saved to be used for a stud fee to a stallion of equal caliber. Though he ached at the thought of eventually selling it, a good price for the foal would go a long way toward securing the farm. Quite a burden for one not yet born.

Peter smiled at the persistent nickering of the barn's other equine residents and the cow's insistent lowing. He turned from the mare to face the others, who watched him with varying degrees of patience. "I'd be flattered, but I know your greeting isn't because you're happy to see me, but because you want what I can do for you."

Following a final pat on Bella's sleek neck, Peter went to the feed room to measure out breakfast for the multiple horses waiting eagerly behind stall doors. Whether they appreciated it or not, each one received a few pats along with their meal.

The Ayrshire cow continually protested the order of service.

"You're next, Clover. When have I ever forgotten you?" Peter reassured the cow as he eased back the hatch that opened into the barn's adjacent concrete block silo. When, even with the door fully extended, nothing spilled into the receiving cart below the hatch, he squatted to peer inside the small opening.

Peter groaned as he stared up into the tall, cavernous cylinder. Along the far wall was a large, consolidated mass of corn. So large it included in its length the lower section of the rusty metal ladder that, bolted to the wall, provided entry into the silo. Golden yellow, the mass looked like a huge elongated honeycomb. But there was nothing sweet about it.

He grimaced. Apparently last fall, distracted by Lucetta's abrupt abandonment, he'd harvested the corn with too much moisture in it. Cautiously poking his head into the hatch, Peter sniffed, detecting only the odor of grain dust and thankfully, not mold.

Ever since a childhood case of pneumonia, breathing in mold had set his lungs off. Fortunately, the corn hadn't been wet enough for that. Only wet enough to stick together when crowded and stored in the silo. The cow and hogs could still eat it, a major comfort to his finances. The mass was just temporarily and—Peter eyed its unwieldy length that looked like it could fall at any moment—dangerously out of reach. Hopefully gravity would soon bring it down by itself.

Peter ducked back out and closed the hatch. Frowning at the Ayrshire, he calculated adjustments to her feed until he could address the consolidated corn. Having done so, he made short work of milking her, mixed some of the milk with oats for the two eager hogs and filtered the rest into a milk can.

Setting the milk can at the barn door, Peter narrowed his eyes at the house before shifting them to the patiently waiting bay at the hitching post. He sighed. Where to put the schoolteacher's horse? He had room in the barn. But arranging for the mare established some sense of permanency. Something he'd rather her mistress not have in his life. That *any* female, other than his daughters and his horses, not have in his life.

He had permanency with Lucetta. An empty one. That part of his life was just an unending... void.

But one that left an open stall. The school-teacher's mare would stay where Lucetta's Standardbred had resided, the one she'd cattily campaigned for, even though he'd always ensured Hazel had been available for her use. A temporary place for temporary women.

Lucetta hadn't needed the horse for the nights she'd snuck out. Someone had picked her up at the end of their lane on those evenings. Peter had sold the horse, along with the extra buggy, when it was obvious Lucetta wasn't coming back. He'd waited a month before doing so. Just to be sure. He couldn't afford to reacquire them. The money had gone to needed farm expenses and to hire a local community woman to make some new dresses for the girls.

Though he and Lucetta had become no more than stiff neighbors, with her in the house and him in the *daadi haus*, Peter had been gutted at being left for another man. Gutted at knowing the whole community was aware of her desertion. Living separately on the same property was one thing. Total abandonment was another. For weeks after she'd disappeared, Peter had flinched every time he heard a horse, or car, come in the lane. Was Lucetta returning? Did he want her to?

Though even now the prospect made his stomach twist, there was no doubt he'd take her back if she did. He'd made a vow before *Gott* and the district. Lucetta was his wife and always would be. Divorce wasn't an option. But was it better that she stayed away and left him and his daughters in limbo, with him in it for life? After the initial bewilderment, the girls seemed happier, less anxious, than when their peevish and critical *mamm* was around. No question about it, except for creating a childcare dilemma, Lucetta's departure was *gut* for the girls.

And for him? A part of him was relieved she'd left. The part that wasn't numb. The part that wasn't suspicious now of every woman's motives, resentful of the members in the community who were curious and ashamed to receive the compassion of the rest.

Peter climbed up to the hayloft to toss straw down for bedding. The numb part wondered what had gone so wrong from the dreams and expectations he'd had of what a marriage would be. What it should be. A marriage like his parents had. One of partnership. Of mutual respect.

He rubbed a hand across the back of his neck. Was he the one who'd failed it? *Ja*, once they were married, Lucetta was not the woman he thought she was. But as a man, he was head of the household. With that came responsibilities. Biblical, financial, emotional, physical ones.

Peter watched the last of the straw flutter down to the barn floor. According to Lucetta, he'd failed at every one of them. Had the fault all been his? Perhaps it was a *gut* thing he was uselessly tied to Lucetta. This way, he wouldn't have the chance to marry another and find out that it was.

After finishing in the barn and the nearby chicken coop, Peter carried the milk can as far as the porch. He listened for a moment to the muted sound of water running in the sink, the rattle of dishes, and the cheerful murmur of voices. Heat crept up the back of his neck. It was obvious that there was a lot more than just the breakfast dishes that needed washing. He almost stepped into the kitchen to apologize. But if he did, the teacher would probably respond. And he'd be expected to say something back. *Nee*, better to just leave it for now.

Peter froze as footsteps headed toward the back door beside him. A bead of sweat trickled down his back at being caught lurking outside the door. Quietly retreating, he unhitched the schoolteacher's mare and took her to the barn where he unharnessed her and harnessed a couple of the draft horses. When he directed the team out the big double doors to hitch to the corn planter, Bella neighed as if to complain about being left behind.

"We'll be back," he called through the doors

he'd left open to the fine spring weather. As he attached the planter's neck yoke to the Belgians' harnesses, the routine and anticipated peace of the workday ahead settled over him. Peter cast a final glance toward the house before firmly pushing the intruding woman from his mind.

Several hours later the sweat-stained Belgians deviated from their steady field pace to pull eagerly as they headed toward the barn for the midday break and a bite to eat. Having missed breakfast, Peter understood their enthusiasm. He was so hungry it felt like his stomach was shaking hands with his backbone.

There wasn't any movement from the house as he unhooked the planter and directed the draft team into the barn, although he thought he saw a face in the window in one of his many surreptitious glances that way. Was the teacher a good cook? His stomach growled at the possibility. Surely anything she prepared would be better than the sandwiches he had slapped together for himself at noon breaks when the girls had been at Lydia's. Even if it was just a sandwich, it probably wouldn't be proper to grab it and retreat back to the porch or barn like he wanted to. He couldn't do that to his girls. Had she already fed them? Hopefully there were leftovers.

Peter's hunger almost urged him into a trot to

the house. But the prospect of sitting at the table with the schoolteacher for the duration of a meal had him dragging his feet. Stepping through the back door into the mudroom, he closed his eyes and inhaled so deeply his suspenders threatened to snap. The aroma of a home-cooked meal. How long had it been since there'd been something besides sandwiches, fried eggs and potatoes or oatmeal prepared in this house?

He stepped forward, bumping into the milk can, now empty and clean, something he'd previously had to do himself.

Malinda, her hair neatly combed and tucked into a *kapp*, popped into the doorway to the kitchen. "*Daed*, you need to wash up. It's almost time for dinner. And we helped!" The last was exclaimed as if it was a special treat.

Fannie appeared beside her, her grin as white as the miniature apron she wore over her dress. "*Ja! Kumme* eat!"

Setting his hat on a nearby wall peg, Peter followed them into the kitchen, his attention drawn to the basket of biscuits and steaming casserole on the table. A table loaded with dinnerware and food. Underlying the aroma of the casserole was a whiff of vinegar. The previously crowded counter had been cleared to reveal its worn—but now clean—laminate surface.

Embarrassment flamed Peter's cheeks that

she'd had to clean up the mess. His mess. He crossed his arms over his chest. "I hired you to take care of my girls. Not clean the house."

Grace turned from where she was filling glasses of water at the sink. Her initial smile faded at his glower. Malinda and Fannie's expressions wilted as well. Peter's stomach twisted at having sunk their joy into the cavernous black hole he'd become. He dropped fisted hands to his side. Despite the tantalizing aromas and his gnawing hunger, he almost retreated to the barn. After a few heartbeats of heavy silence in the room, Peter flinched when Fannie reached out to grab his wrist.

"We helped." Her voice was as small as her size.

Looking into his *dochter*'s earnest eyes, Peter struggled to swallow past the lump in his throat. "You…you all did a *gut* job," he finally rasped. He hissed in a breath at seeing her grin resurrected. "Dinner looks and smells *gut* too." At Malinda's tentative smile, he tried a stiff one of his own. "I'll just get washed up like you suggested." Ducking his head, Peter spun on his heel and escaped to the washroom.

He avoided his reflection in the small mirror as he washed the field dust from his face. *You coward. Your lack of joy doesn't excuse stealing their chance for it. Just because Lucetta poisoned your well doesn't mean you have to poison theirs.* While swiping the hand towel over his face, he paused to press it momentarily over closed eyes. *Gott, please help me be the father my daughters need.*

His girls and the schoolteacher were already at the table when he returned to the kitchen. After a silent prayer, the girls watched him expectantly as he took a bite.

"Mmm," he groaned appreciatively. "When did you girls learn to be such *gut* cooks?"

"Grace did most of it," Malinda admitted. Still, she brightened at his words.

"I found the noodles," Fannie added.

"Must've been quite the hunt." Peter winked at her, though he chewed his bite of casserole more vigorously than it warranted as he recalled the kitchen's regrettable condition.

There was no sound for several minutes but the scrape of cutlery on dinnerware. Grace, wearing a hesitant smile, tipped her head toward the one area at the end of the counter on which a number of items were stacked.

"I wasn't sure where they went."

Peter stopped chewing as he gazed at the items she'd indicated. If they were things of Lucetta's, he was tempted to have them thrown out, just as she'd tossed him and his daughters aside. But he'd never do that when something could prove useful.

They might be items the girls would want later. Or—Peter had to force the food past the sudden knot in his throat—something that Lucetta would complain was missing if she ever came back.

"Just put them wherever makes sense and there's room."

Grace nodded. Her tentative smile widened. To avoid it, Peter dropped his gaze to stab another forkful of noodles.

"I didn't see a garden started." Grace's voice rose at the end, like it was a question.

Peter's tension rose with it. His head jerked up. Coming from Lucetta, the statement would've been an accusation. Instead of Grace's soft lilt, Lucetta would've escalated to a yell if the words were not otherwise pitted with sarcasm. His shoulders automatically tightened as if they were being pulled up to his ears.

He hadn't gotten around to putting in a garden this spring. He'd planted them in previous years only to watch the untended plants get choked out by weeds due to Lucetta's lack of interest or effort. Peter liked fresh vegetables and the self-sufficiency and economy of growing his own food. But by himself, he wouldn't have time for it this year, so he'd reluctantly let it go.

"It's not too late to plant."

He gritted his teeth. The schoolteacher hadn't even been here a full day, and already she was finding fault with him. Lucetta had frequently insinuated that he wasn't working hard enough to suit her.

Not bothering with insinuations, the school-teacher went straight to criticism.

Well, he could be direct as well. "Wasn't planning on putting in a garden this year." He chomped down on a biscuit, biting it in two and chewing mechanically.

Grace studied him as she set her silverware onto her plate. "I see." Apparently, she could read his jutted chin and compressed lips as well as the school primers she taught from. "I guess when the produce markets open, the girls and I can make some trips to see what's available. And folks always have a few extra zucchini and summer squash to share once those seasons start."

Peter's chin lifted higher. "We don't need charity from our neighbors. Things might be...tight, but I can afford to feed my family."

Grace lifted her brow. She glanced to where Malinda and Fannie's wide eyes were following the conversation before returning her gaze to him. "I can see you take *gut* care of your girls."

Peter's eyes narrowed. Was she being sarcastic? If Lucetta had spoken the words, they would've been weighted with mockery. Under his glare, Grace, smiling faintly, stood and carried her plate to the counter. Peter remained stationary, braced for a renewed attack. When none occurred, only sounds of water filling the sink and the slurp of Fannie taking a drink from her glass, the tightness slowly eased from Peter's shoulders. He slid his chair back and pushed to his feet. Snagging his hat as he passed, Peter grimly tugged down on the worn straw brim as he went out the door. His stomach might be comfortably full having a woman in his kitchen again, but his mind was poisoned by the memories of the last one who'd been there.

Watching Peter's stiff back as he marched to the barn, Grace was tempted to do something she'd never done before—count the days until school started again. If every dinner this summer was going to be as strained as this one, maybe she would take her chances and go home to Iowa. She glanced down at the rattling noise near her hip to see Fannie holding up a plate, a fork perched precariously on top. Malinda was a step behind her, similarly laden.

"*Denki*, girls," Grace murmured, relieving them of their burdens with a smile. She watched as they skipped back to the table for another load.

During the morning, they'd gradually relaxed, unfurling like tightly held buds blighted by cold when spring finally arrived. Not that she likened herself to spring, but from what she'd heard in the community and the actions of the girls—and their father—she was at least a February thaw compared to what they'd had before. *Nee*, maybe she would have to resort to counting the days because of their *daed*, but she wouldn't leave these little ones.

The girls pulled a couple of chairs over to help with the dishes. Their assistance made things take longer, but as their father had chided, she'd been hired to care for them, not the house. Still, as she assisted Fannie with folding a damp dishcloth over the stove handle, she stared into the living area with a frown.

"Now that, thanks to your help, we have the kitchen in better shape, let's see what we can do in there, *ja*?"

Malinda and Fannie didn't hesitate to agree. That task and cleaning the girls' bedroom was what they spent the afternoon on. As the day wore on, the little ones' enthusiasm wilted. Grace left them to play on the front porch while she organized the kitchen to find a place for the stacked items on the counter. She was shelving the final object when she heard Fannie holler.

"*Daed* has harnessed Bella! Where's he going?"

Grace looked out the screen door. Peter was indeed crossing the farmyard behind a huge chestnut Belgian mare, a one bottom plow almost gg/

looking like a toy as it rattled across the gravel behind her. Grace stepped outside to join the girls. Fannie immediately reached for her hand.

"He's going to plow the garden. That's a walking plow. He uses the riding plow if he's working in the fields. And at least two horses, with one walking in the furrow and one on the unplowed ground."

Grace glanced in surprise at Malinda's confident explanation. "How do you know so much?"

"*Daed* would sometimes take us to the field before our *mamm* left if she wanted him to. We'd play in the end rows while he did the fieldwork. When he rested the horses after each round, he'd explain what he was doing while we got to sit on them. When I get bigger, I'm going to help him."

Grace smiled at the little girl's determined expression. "I'm sure you will."

Fannie tugged on Grace's apron. "Can we go watch?"

"Sounds like a *gut* idea. As long as we stay out of the way. That is a big horse."

"She's the best. But some of her bigness is because she's going to have a *boppeli*. It's going to be worth a lot of money. And *Daed*'s going to train it and then sell it. Or maybe just sell it when it's weaned. Depending on what the market is."

The normally quieter Malinda, obviously fond of horses, was a wealth of information as they followed Peter and the mare beyond the yard. The girls, having gone without shoes for some time that spring, showed no indication the gravel bothered their bare feet. But Grace, who'd until recently been wearing shoes to school, caught herself wincing as she minced across the rocks.

Peter looked back. Grace bit her lip, prepared to return to the house in case he waved them off. But he turned around without a word. He and the mare continued to a broad patch of ground, the tangle of weeds and lighter soil differentiating it from the spring-green carpet of grass that bordered its square shape.

Grace's steps quickened when she noticed short stocky spears poking up through a tangle of dried yellow stalks. "You have an asparagus patch."

The big mare halted nearby at a single word from Peter. "My uncle started it some years ago. It needs work." His jaw firmed when her gaze moved from him to the plow.

"I've kept Bella pretty quiet with the upcoming arrival of the foal. She needed the exercise."

Though Grace nodded solemnly, she bit the inside of her cheek at what she knew was an excuse. Or perhaps some form of apology?

Peter eyed her placid expression before turning his attention to the plow. He toed in the blade, ensured the Belgian's reins were secure around his body, gripped the plow's high wooden handles and instructed the mare to "walk on." She did so, as the single blade dug into the soil. It seemed to take more time to turn the rig around at the far end and situate the plow for the return trip than it did to make the trip across the garden. Before the first furrow was complete, the girls were scrambling over the turned earth like it was a favored playground.

"I found one!"

Grace looked over from where she'd been inspecting the asparagus patch. One what? Malinda's exuberant shriek could've announced any kind of fantastic discoveries. Maybe there was some kind of forgotten *Englisch* treasure buried in the garden. Fannie scurried over the spaded ground to join her sister. Inhaling sharply, Grace pressed her hand to her chest at the heartwarming sight of the girls acting like excited children instead of dutiful miniature adults.

"Daed! Daed! Look!"

Peter turned back toward his daughters. The big mare stopped abruptly at his quiet "Whoa."

Malinda shot her hand into the air. Grace squinted to see what she was holding.

"Oh my," she murmured at the sight of a long worm dangling from the girl's dainty fingers.

Malinda carried her prize over and thrust it toward Grace. "Are you afraid of worms?"

Grace grinned. She'd become inured over the past few school years to all the creepy crawly things that young boys had brought into the one-room school. "*Nee*. There are things that I'm afraid of." Like having to return to Iowa, where she knew she'd succumb to her *mamm*'s pressure. "But worms aren't one of them."

Good thing, as a moment later, Fannie thrust her hand forward, a squirming large earthworm covering the whole surface of her tiny palm. After Grace's admiration of their finds, the girls raced over to show their *daed*.

"You've got some fine fat ones there. They're probably pretty shocked to have their homes disturbed. I imagine you'll find others as well as I plow up the rest of this."

"If we do, can we go fishing?"

Efficiently lining the mare up for another pass of the garden patch, Peter puckered his brow as he considered Malinda's request. "*Ja*. Get a can for the worms. Don't forget to put in a little dirt to keep them happy. I'll finish this, put Bella up, and do chores. Then we'll see if any fish are hungry." He set the plow and instructed Bella to "walk on" once again. The harness rattled as the big mare moved out. His broad back stiffened when Fannie called after him.

"Can Grace come too?"

Chapter Five

Peter abruptly stopped. The big mare, still moving along the plowed furrow, jerked him forward.

"Whoa," he blurted belatedly, and the huge haunches immediately halted before him.

He rubbed a hand across the back of his neck as he turned to regard Fannie. "Grace has already put in quite a long first day. I'm sure she has things she wants to get home to." His blue eyes lifted to narrow on Grace, clearly chiding her for his daughter's invitation.

Fannie tugged on Grace's skirt with dirt-streaked fingers. "Do you have things you want to get home to?"

Grace ducked her head to hide her grin. Peter wanted her to say she had to go home. It was obvious he couldn't wait to see the back end of her buggy as it rolled down the lane. But to Fannie's question, she really didn't have anything to go home to. Just a silent little house that she was allocated along with her job. No papers to grade.

No animals but the horse to tend to. No letters to write beyond the one she wanted to avoid. The one informing her *mamm* she wouldn't be returning to Iowa for the summer. The one sure to set off another response from her parent. *Nee*, she'd rather avoid going home to face that task.

Even though it had been a long day, particularly after her five o'clock arrival, the evenings were long this time of year. Long and lonely. Though she needed to retire early to be here tomorrow again at five, it was difficult to go to bed when the sun was still up. It'd been fun today with the two girls. She wasn't quite ready for it to end.

Besides, their father so clearly wanted her to say no. Why did that tempt her so?

"What a wonderful idea. I used to fish when I was little too." Grace smiled at Fannie. "Where do you go for your hungry fish?"

Malinda looked up from where she was brushing soil away to unearth the rest of a fat worm. "There's a sinkhole back in the pasture. When the river floods over it, sometimes fish get in there. When the river goes back into its banks, they can't get out."

"They get stuck. Because they're foolish." Fannie added. "And then we catch them."

"It sounds like fun. Maybe I could even catch a foolish fish." Grace glanced at Peter in time to see a knot flex in his jaw. For a moment, she took pity on him. "But I don't have a pole."

Malinda stood, holding her captured worm in one hand while she swiped the other across her apron. "That's all right. We have extra. As long as you don't mind old bamboo ones."

"It's what I learned to fish with. If I'm to join you, maybe I can pack a picnic while your *daed* does chores. Because, even if the fish aren't hungry, for sure and certain, I am."

Fannie's face seemed almost too small to contain her wide smile. "That would be *wunderbar*!" She pivoted and raced toward the house. "I'll find a can for the worms!" she called over her shoulder.

Malinda sprinted after her. "I'll get the poles out. I know where they are." Their little legs and bare feet, already tanning from time spent outside, dashed over the green grass.

Grace winced as she watched them race toward the house. Hopefully in their enthusiasm they didn't squish the worms in their hands. She turned to face their father and bit her lip. Definitely no enthusiasm there at the impromptu plans for the evening.

"Shall I follow and tell them no?"

His gaze, too, turned toward the racing girls. He scowled. "Too late now." Sighing, he scrubbed a hand over his face. "It'll take me about an hour to finish this and do chores."

"Anything we can do to help?"

He eyed her as if judging her sincerity. "You ever feed chickens? Gather eggs from under broody hens?"

"Oh, is that where they come from?" Grace responded sweetly.

Her brows lifted when his lips thinned sharply at her jest. A ripple of shame swept through her. It was obvious the man worked hard and cared greatly for his daughters. Just because he was as prickly as a cocklebur didn't mean she should tease him. Grace cleared her throat as she remembered his missing wife. She hadn't known the woman, but she'd heard rumors. Perhaps the man had reason to be sensitive.

"*Ja.* I have. Does Malinda know where the feed and the egg baskets are?" At his nod, she continued. "Then I'm sure the girls and I can handle it. In fact, the three of us can take on that chore from now on. It will be *gut* for them."

Peter frowned. "They might be afraid of the hens. Due to…past history."

"I was, too, when I was little. Don't worry. I'll make sure if anyone is pecked, it's me."

"I hope that doesn't happen. I can't afford to have any of my flock poisoned." Though his expression remained stoic, Peter's eyes glinted.

Turning toward the mare, he took hold of the plow's wooden handles.

Staring at his back, Grace stifled a snort. Humor from him? Directed at her? If so, it was as barbed as the rest of him. "I'll make sure I have a picnic ready by the time you're finished."

Peter grunted in acknowledgment. The big mare lurched forward at his command and they pulled away, leaving another row of spaded earth behind them.

"And any extra worms that are found, I'll put in your sandwich," Grace murmured to his departing back.

"What was that?"

She jumped at the words spoken from almost underfoot. Fannie was at her elbow, a can they'd emptied for dinner that day gripped in her hand. How had she returned so quickly? Grace bit her tongue as her cheeks heated. She knew from teaching that little pitchers had big ears. The girls were delightful, but anything she said might get back to their father. She forced a smile. "I said let's get some extra worms, then I'll go make sandwiches."

Fannie—looking remarkably like her father as she did so—eyed her suspiciously, obviously noting the difference between the two comments. Grace's flush spread. *Day one on the job and I'm lying to the children.* Putting her words into practice, she squatted in the churned up ground beside the girl, and along with Malinda, when she returned with a few long-faded yellow poles, they coaxed worms from the freshly turned soil until the can was two-thirds full of the squirming creatures.

As he directed the mare into another turn at the far end of the garden plot, Peter sighed as he watched the trio parade to the house. More hours with the schoolteacher. *Ach*, at least since she would be busy helping the girls fish, he wouldn't have to make conversation with her.

Had she coached Fannie to ask to include her in the activity? It was possible. The woman had been sly enough to manipulate Miriam and Lydia into helping her get this job.

She said she'd fished when she was young. An image of a pretty blond-haired girl with big blue eyes popped into his head. One with a sunny nature and a constantly clean apron. Peter scowled. He didn't want to think of Grace as a little girl like his daughters. He was having a difficult enough time ignoring her as a young woman. A beautiful young woman. One he needed to evict from his mind.

Peter grunted as his shoulder slammed into the handle when the plow blade jolted against a big rock. Wincing at the new ache, he halted Bella with a word and bent to dig around the stone with his hands and wiggle it until he freed it from its berth. He hefted it with a groan and carried it to the edge of the plot to toss aside. Brushing the dirt from his hands, Peter returned to the patiently waiting mare. That's what he needed to remember. However weedy and disreputable the garden of his life was, the teacher—no matter how pretty and …pleasant—was a rock in it. One that needed to be removed for the overall health of the garden before he kept stumbling over it.

He wrapped the long reins about his shoulders. "Walk on, Bella."

And here he was. Thinking of her again.

He'd opened his mouth to say no to Fannie's request until he saw his *dochter*'s face. When he couldn't outright deny his little girl, he'd willed the schoolteacher to decline. Which had been a futile exercise. Peter turned the mare again and started another furrow. But no more futile than plowing a garden that wouldn't be used. But one he had time today to plow because he didn't have to worry about making supper tonight, as there were ample leftovers from dinner. A dinner he hadn't had to make, in a kitchen that was as clean as it had been in months, if not longer. All because of the schoolteacher.

Ach, he'd be too busy baiting hooks, helping the girls cast and retrieve their lines to worry about talking. And if the girls were doing all right by themselves, he could move on down the bank.

Let the teacher come.

As he came back on the final row, Peter saw Grace and his girls, egg basket in Fannie's hand, cross the farmyard toward the chicken run. Fannie slowed before stopping altogether as they approached the coop. Peter frowned as Grace retraced her steps to the lagging little girl. His muscles tightened. He'd cross the distance in an instant if the teacher made any move to drag his reluctant daughter toward the coop.

To his surprise, Grace squatted beside the girl. They had a short conversation before the teacher stood and relieved Fannie of her basket. Fannie skipped over to a tree swing in the yard and sat down. Malinda and Grace entered the barn, reappearing after a moment with a small bucket of feed. While Malinda tossed handfuls of grain into the chicken run, Grace went into the coop alone with the basket.

Having reached the edge of the garden, Peter furrowed his brow as he freed the blade from the soil. Lucetta had always sent the girls to do the chicken chores. He'd quietly taken over after noticing blue peck-mark bruises from cantankerous hens on their slender arms. Neither he nor the girls had said a word to Lucetta about transferring the chore. No one wanted to face the resulting outburst. He probably should've coached the girls on how to deal with the hens. They needed to learn responsibility. But they'd proven to be very responsible over their brief years without the help of poultry. So he'd just added tending the chickens to his own chores.

Grace emerged from the coop, egg-laden basket in hand. Fannie left her perch on the swing and skipped over to retrieve it from Grace. Tipped lop-sided by her heavy burden, his younger daughter carried the basket toward the house while Malinda returned the feed bucket to the barn and trotted to catch up. Peter watched thoughtfully as they disappeared into the house.

"Race you!" Fannie challenged Malinda before dashing toward where mature oaks shaded the far end of the horse pasture. Before Peter could voice an objection, the girls sprinted ahead. Leaving him—laden with poles, stringer and the can of worms—alone with the schoolteacher. Straightening his shoulders, he kept his gaze on his racing daughters while every other bit of attention was on the lithe woman walking beside him, picnic basket in hand.

Oddly enough, now that they were on their way to the fishing hole, he didn't resent Grace joining for what had always been he and the girls' private outings. Lucetta had never gone fishing with them. The three fishermen had all been relieved to have time away from her. Since Lucetta had left, what with taking and fetching the girls from Lydia's place in addition to his farm work, there hadn't been time to fish.

But now there was. Because of Grace.

For several moments, the only sound was the swish of their feet walking through the lush spring grass. Peter cleared his throat. "So, you've fished before?"

"Oh, *ja*. The Iowa River ran through a bit of our property. My siblings and I would hurry through chores and, along with occasional neighbor children, go to the river to do a bit of fishing. I was happy to catch all but one kind." She wrinkled her nose. "Once, a neighbor boy tried to put a small catfish down the back of my dress. I never liked them after that."

"The boy or the fish?"

She grinned. "Neither for a while." Her smile faded. "I grew to like the boy in later years. It would've been wiser to have reconciled to the fish instead."

Peter found himself nodding in agreement. How different his life might've been if he'd gone fishing with new friends in the Miller's Creek community instead of immediately becoming enamored with a girl who'd been sending out her own lures. Like the girls had said earlier about the sinkholes, he'd hung around when he shouldn't have and been caught like those fish—because he'd been foolish.

"Over here!"

At Malinda's call, they veered toward where she and Fannie were stomping down the grass on the bank of a small pond. Bugs flitted across the dark green surface. As he and Grace approached, a fish jumped out of the water after an unsuspecting insect. It splashed down again, creating circles that expanded over the pond.

Fannie pointed a little finger. "See! There are hungry fish in there."

"We made a picnic spot," Malinda indicated the flattened grass where she and her sister had been tromping. "Or we can have it on the sandbar." She pointed to a slender stretch of sand and gravel about twenty yards away that fringed the Fox River. The river, still slightly swollen with spring rains and snowmelt, lumbered by with a quiet murmur.

Peter glanced at Grace, allocating the decision to her. He was startled at the ripple of delight— or was it unease?—that swept through him when she smiled and nodded.

"I think you've made a lovely spot here." She set the picnic basket down.

Wary of either source of the ripple, Peter moved farther along the bank before stooping to set down the can of worms and the poles. "How about you girls get the picnic started while I prepare our gear?"

"Sounds like a *gut* plan."

Another ripple rolled through him when Grace endorsed his suggestion. A rare occurrence in his married life. He glanced over to see if she was mocking him, but her attention was on the contents of the picnic basket as she retrieved a church spread sandwich for Fannie and a cheese one for Malinda.

A warmth unrelated to the long spring evening crept over him as Peter ensured each thin fishing line had a small weight secured to sink the hook into the water and that the round red-and-white bobbers were set at an appropriate length. Preparations complete, he joined the trio sitting around a red-and-white-checkered tablecloth as they ate their sandwiches.

"Got one for me?"

"Of course." Grace pulled out another sandwich and handed it to him.

He took a big bite, his eyes closing in appreciation at the taste of fresh bread.

"She said she was going to put worms in your sandwich, *Daed*."

Peter's eyes popped open as he stopped chewing at Fannie's words. And made sure to carefully taste every aspect of what was in his mouth.

Bread. Cheese. Mayonnaise. He rolled the food around on his tongue, relieved that the final and only additional flavor he recognized was…ham?

Glancing down, he saw Grace's face was as red as the checkered cloth under her knee.

"I… I…well… I…but…" she sputtered.

"Hmm. If she did, they were tasty ones. Shall we see?" He squatted to the girls' level. On their tiptoes, Fannie and Malinda leaned against his knee for a better look as he slowly peeled the top piece of bread from the sandwich. When he carefully lifted each layer of the sandwich to reveal only ham and cheese smeared with mayonnaise, the girls eased back on their heels and sighed in seeming disappointment.

"Well, she did say it," Fannie maintained.

Grace, still so flushed the center part of her blond hair was a bright red strip, to his surprise, confessed. "I did. I was…teasing."

Peter eyed her as he took a few more bites of the now safe sandwich. It'd been a long time since he'd been teased, not mocked, by a woman. It caused…more ripples. Bigger ones. Ones he didn't want to think about. Grace looked like she'd like to jump into the nearby pond and not surface for a long time. He took pity on her.

"I'm glad she didn't. What a waste of worms that would've been. We need them for fishing."

Finishing the sandwich, he brushed the crumbs from his hands. "Are you ready?"

In answer, the girls scrambled to their feet. Grace kept her head down as she collected picnic remnants and returned them to the basket. But as he led his daughters to where he'd left the poles, he intercepted a glance from her. The color in Grace's cheeks was still heightened, but she smiled and rolled her eyes.

To his surprise, Peter found himself smiling back.

As he looked back across the pond, his eyes blurred for a moment and he rapidly blinked as he hissed in a breath. He slowed to a halt, which the girls took as an invitation to take his hands, one in each of their own. Peter curled his calloused fingers about their miniature ones. This is what he'd grown up with. What he'd envisioned a marriage partnership to be. What he'd wished for his children. A family outing where there were no strained or yelling voices. No hunched shoulders or chilly silences. No wary, darting glances from the girls. Just happy, excited chatter. Gentle teasing. Shared smiles. A wife preparing and setting out a picnic while he tended to fishing poles. He glanced again to where Grace was folding up the checkered tablecloth. His smile faded.

But he had a wife. Somewhere. A wife, even

if she returned, with whom it was doubtful this enjoyable scene would ever occur.

"Which pole is mine?"

Relieved that Fannie's question interrupted his dark thoughts, Peter released her grasp to pass her the shortest of the three. The next several minutes were consumed with threading worms on hooks and helping little hands swing the lines across the water to let bobbers plop gently onto its surface. In Fannie's case, it included wrapping his hand around the end of the long bamboo as hers alone couldn't keep the pole steady enough to prevent its tip from dipping into the water.

It was quiet except for the subdued hum of insects that drifted over the pond. As Peter knelt beside Fannie, helping to hold her pole, he looked out across the pasture toward the farmstead. His farmstead. From here, he couldn't see buildings that needed to be painted or the oft-repaired fences. From a distance, it looked like a thriving establishment. The corners of his mouth tipped up as he considered his farm. There was an odd sensation that felt just out of reach. As if it, were he to extend a hand and try to grab it, would disappear.

"*Daed*, I think I got one." Malinda's tone was hushed as her red-and-white-bobber bounced on the pond's surface, sending ripples rolling across the dark green water. "*Daed. Daed!*" She quickly escalated from whisper to shriek as the bobber submerged completely and the tip of the yellow bamboo arched toward the water.

Peter tried to reach for her pole while still keeping a hand on Fannie's.

"Help, *Daed*!" At Malinda's yelp, he let go of Fannie's pole. Now on her own with the unwieldy fishing gear, his younger daughter was jerked closer to the edge of the bank as the long pole swung down toward the water. Peter, arms stretched wide, was caught between the two.

Then Grace was there.

"Here we go." Wrapping her arms about Fannie, she drew the little girl from the pond's edge and helped her raise the pole back into position.

Peter squatted by Malinda's side and joined her small hands on the bamboo. "Ready?" At her nod, they jerked the pole upward to see a tall, flat fish launch out of the water.

"You caught a bluegill!" Together, they maneuvered the pole so the line and flapping fish swung to the bank.

"Let me see!" Fannie abandoned her own pole to hurry over. Peter looked up from where he'd grasped the landed fish to see that Grace had everything there under control. The girls rested their hands on his shoulders as Peter squatted to remove the hook from the bluegill's small mouth and put the fish on the stringer. They stretched out a hand to touch its slippery side before Peter slid it back into the water.

"Looks like we'll be having fish for dinner tomorrow. *If* someone will clean it. Which is where I draw the line." Grace was dubiously eyeing the empty hook on Fannie's pole. "And either this worm was *gut* at escaping, or there are some particularly smart fish in this pond."

"Of course they're smart."

"Oh, why's that?" Grace looked over expectantly.

"Because they're in a school." Malinda giggled at her own joke. When Peter snorted and shook his head, she doubled over with laughter. Fannie, despite not understanding the joke, joined in.

Peter's heart surged at his daughters' spontaneous delight, a rarity indeed. His gaze lifted to meet Grace's. The earlier ripples now rolled through him like waves.

"I want to catch one!" Fannie hurriedly retrieved her pole from Grace and attempted to wrestle the line back into the water. The other three jerked out of the way as the empty hook flew over their heads. Grabbing the bamboo, Grace steadied it until she could secure the line.

"Be careful," Peter reminded his *dochter*. "And hold on a moment. We've got to bait it first." He rummaged in the can for a worm and brought it over. As Grace slid her fingers down the thin nylon line, Peter reached for the dangling hook. Concentrating on their tasks, their fingertips touched. And lingered. Peter's heart stopped as he felt, more than heard, Grace's soft gasp. Breath held, he stared into her blue eyes, sharing her equally startled gaze. For a moment, neither of them moved.

He dropped the earthworm. No fool, it wiggled deeper into the lush spring grass.

"*Daed!* He's getting away!"

Peter blinked at Malinda's urgent warning. He jerked his fingers away and dropped his hand to comb the grass, searching for the fugitive worm. *At least the worm was smart enough to try to escape. I'm more of a fool than that four-inch creature. I don't know enough to scurry away before getting hooked again. And I* am *hooked. Hooked for a lifetime to someone else.* Still, he couldn't prevent a surreptitious glance in Grace's direction, one long enough to note her flushed cheeks, before making a big production out of digging into the can for another worm.

"*Ach*, sorry. Looks like that one will need to be recaptured for a future day of fishing."

"Does that mean we can do this again soon?"

Peter paused. With Grace fixing meals and not having to go back and forth from Lydia's, they indeed might have more time for fishing. "I suppose so, Malinda. If I can get the fieldwork done."

"And Grace can come too?"

Peter looked over at the schoolteacher. He wanted to deny Fannie's request. But how could he when his daughters were looking so hopeful, and Grace was the one who made the outings possible? *"Ja,"* he agreed heavily. "Grace can come too. If she wants," he hastily added.

"Oh, she likes fishing. She'll want to."

Peter forced a smile at Fannie's assurance. He was afraid the problem wouldn't be Grace's wants regarding fishing. It would be his unexpected, unwelcome and unrealistic wants regarding Grace.

Chapter Six

The sun was still just a promise over the horizon as Grace slowed her mare to turn into Peter's lane the next morning. She shifted on the leather buggy seat, trying to relax her shoulders. She'd already had a full day on this new job. The *kinner* were sweet and cooperative. Her nerves should be more settled than they'd been yesterday morning.

Instead, they were jumping like grasshoppers in August.

Oh, Grace. What have you gotten yourself into? If a prickly Peter was annoying, an approachable one was… Grace scrubbed at the goose bumps that abruptly rose under the cotton sleeves of her dress. An approachable Peter was bemusing. Bemusing and…very attractive. Oh, this was awful. She was not one of her older female students mooning over the opposite sex, particularly when it was her new employer. But her wayward goose bumps, stomach flutters and sporadic heartfelt sighs didn't seem to be making the distinction. *What if I make calf eyes at him? What if he catches me doing so?*

Grace groaned. Yesterday when their fingers unexpectedly touched, something had leapt in her like the foolish fish that had jumped out of the pond. How could she now act normally around him?

Her expression immediately sobered. She could, because the man was already married. He was not, and would never be, available to her. Though the current situation made it easier to forget, just because Peter's wife wasn't around didn't mean she didn't exist.

Calf eyes, or any other similar lapse, would only embarrass her and him. And make it difficult for her to tend to his children, whom she'd already grown to care for. So she would act responsibly. Maturely. If she was smart—Grace wrinkled her nose—which she was upon occasion, she wouldn't go fishing with them again. Nor stay to attend any other family outings. Her shoulders drooped. Even though doing so was much more enjoyable than returning to a lonely little house.

Grace's new resolution didn't stop the flutter that swept through her when, in the increasing light, she saw Peter emerge from the house and start across the farmyard. Her palms started sweating. Was he coming out to greet her? She touched her hair, ensuring it was neatly tucked into her *kapp* before dropping her hand back into her lap.

You'd just resolved to act responsibly. The condition of your hair has no impact on your ability to mind his children. Peter is probably coming out to take your horse to the barn.

But what if he helps me down from the buggy since he's right there? And grasps my sweaty palm.

Her heartbeat accelerating, she slid her hand down the length of her apron. She blinked and abruptly straightened when, halfway across the yard, Peter's limber saunter burst into a dash for the barn. Eyes wide, Grace watched as, reaching the big double doors, he fumbled momentarily with the latch before throwing the doors open and disappearing inside.

Her heart was racing. Were the girls all right? *Nee*, it surely wasn't them, as Peter wouldn't have left them in the barn, particularly at this time of day. Should she drive the mare to the barn to see if she could help or go into the house to check on the girls?

In case her horse would be in the way of whatever was going on in the barn, Grace directed the mare to the hitching post by the yard fence and scrambled down to secure her. She paused, tuning all her attention for any sounds coming from the house. Hearing nothing, she sprinted toward the open barn door, slowing her final approach to a hurried but controlled walk. Upon reaching the open doors, she quietly slipped through.

The barn's interior was even darker than the twilight outside, but the quiet shuffling and thumps from the depths of it advised Grace that the building was well occupied. After a frozen moment, she made out Peter's form hovering by a stall on the far wall, the immense silhouette of one of the draft horses beyond him.

"Is everything all right?" she whispered in the darkness.

"I think so," Peter returned in an equally hushed tone. His attention was on the stall's interior. "I hope so. When I heard the groan, I wasn't sure."

Grace crept closer to peek into the stall herself. At first, she couldn't see anything in the stygian shadows until her eyes followed the big horse's neck to its lowered head. Grace wouldn't have recognized the animal among the others in the barn except for its size. It was the huge mare that had plowed the garden yesterday. Yesterday she'd shown her physical strength. This morning, the mare revealed her maternal ability as she licked and nuzzled a wet foal.

"Oh my." Grace didn't know why she was still whispering. Although she loved and had been around horses all her life, she'd never been present at this stage. "It's so big already. Is it a colt or a filly?"

"It looks like a little colt."

"Did you have a preference on a boy or a girl?"

"I just wanted a healthy one."

Grace cocked her head at the little one, who looked a bit stunned at his new situation as, with a lifted head, he took in his surroundings. "He looks alert enough."

"Ja." Peter never took his eyes off the pair. He stiffened when Bella shifted her attention from the foal to look back at her belly. "A lot of things can still go wrong yet though." When the mare nosed around other parts of the stall and her knees buckled until she laid down on the straw-strewn floor, Peter inched closer to the stall door.

"If Bella starts rolling too much or looking at her belly too often, it could be a sign of colic. If so, I need to get to the phone shack to call a veterinarian. Birthing can be dangerous for both mother and child."

After an anxious moment when the mare rocked almost to her back on the straw-covered floor, the horse lunged upright again and returned to sniffing the new arrival.

"What's wrong with his feet?" Grace pointed to the spongy-looking growths on the foal's miniature hooves. They didn't look like anything she'd ever seen before.

"Those are called hoof slippers. They protect the mare until the foal is born. They usually disappear within a day when the foal gets to walking."

"Which will be soon, right?" To her relief, with all the attention on the occupants of the stall, there was no sign of the awkward tension she'd worried about while coming up the lane. She propped her elbows on the half wall as she watched the pair.

"A foal must stand up within an hour. He needs to nurse soon to help him get the antibodies he needs from his *mamm*."

Peter's fingers curled over the wall's smooth wood, and he rocked up on his toes. He looked like he was almost willing the new baby to get to his feet. Grace furrowed her brow, recalling an earlier conversation with the girls. Malinda had said the foal was important. Peter's anxiety emphasized how much. Grace ached to comfort him. Lifting a hand, she reached over to touch his arm before jerking it higher to flip a dangling *kapp* string over her shoulder, as if that had been her purpose all along. *Responsible. Mature.* Surely there were other ways to ease his stress without creating more—and a potentially dangerous and unwelcome type—of tension.

"What are you going to name him?"

Peter grunted. "I'll leave that to the girls. Within reason. I don't think the one-ton horse that he will grow up to be would welcome a name like Buttercup or Honey or something of that nature."

"I don't know." Grace cocked her head as she watched the colt lurch to stand on gangly legs, making his cream-colored coat more visible. "Due to his sweet features and coloring, I think both kind of suit him."

Peter rolled his eyes. "Don't give the girls any ideas. They'll come up with enough of that type on their own."

His rigid shoulders visibly eased as the foal staggered over to nose and nibble at his mother's flank. Bella encouraged him as best she could to help him find his first meal. Grace smiled when the foal, already the size of a full-grown pony, tottered under his mother's belly. Between the mare's steadiness and gentle nickering and the foal's persistent nudging, the two soon achieved success.

Warmth seeped over Grace at the sight. She flicked a glance toward Peter. They were both leaning over the stall wall, their elbows a hand's breadth apart, as they watched the amazement of new life, one of *Gott*'s many miracles. It was a… special moment to share it with someone. Special to share it with Peter. A fresh crop of goose bumps swept over her arms. Clearing her throat, Grace straightened and took a step, albeit a reluctant one, back.

Shafts of light were now coming through the barn's dusty windows, illuminating specs of dust in their rays. Grace widened her eyes in dismay. "Oh dear! It's getting late. I'd better go check on the girls. They were up much earlier than this yesterday."

Peter's mouth slanted into a half smile. Grace's goose bumps multiplied. "I think that was due to the excitement of your arrival."

She rubbed her hands over her upper arms. "I hope I didn't disappoint."

Peter shifted his attention from the occupants in the stall to her, pinning Grace with the intensity in his blue eyes. "No," he finally responded. It was more of a breath than a word. He held her gaze for a few more heartbeats before, with a frown, he looked back to the mare and foal.

Grace backed away until she bumped into a bale of hay. She pivoted and hurried toward the big double doors, blinking as she left the barn's dimness for the light of the sun that now stretched above the horizon. The day's external glow almost matched Grace's internal one. As she headed for the house, it was hard to tell which was faster, her heart rate or her trotting steps. Catching herself, Grace slowed to a walk. Responsible. Mature. If she couldn't get herself under control, she shouldn't stay. Would she never learn? Falling for a man who ultimately rejected her was far less foolish than falling for one who was already married.

She had her senses corralled by the time Peter came in for breakfast before going into the field. Due to the girls' excitement and chatter—breakfast was delayed while they made a trip to the barn to see the new foal—that meal and dinner were not as awkward as Grace feared. She'd hardly said a word. Much of the discussion was about the new arrival and what his name should be.

Peter had been right. Buttercup and Honey were suggested as possibilities. After several more along that line, options gently vetoed by their father, the girls settled on Tanner—"'cause he's tan"—to which Peter approved. Grace bit back a smile. For sure and certain, he'd probably realized it was the only one mentioned that would allow the colt, when he was an adult, some dignity.

After a brief nod and gruff thanks for dinner, Peter headed back out to the barn. From the kitchen window, Grace watched him hitch a fresh team to the planter and return to the field. Sensing her eyes going dreamy and her mouth softening into a foolish smile, she abruptly schooled her expression and huffed out a breath. She could handle the short meals with Peter in the presence of the girls. But though the day had gone much better than her expectations this morning, she didn't dare risk any more time with Peter than was necessary. Her determination to be responsible and mature was woefully shaky. Grace resolved that if he was out of the house, she needed to be in it. If he was in it, she needed to be out.

When Peter returned to the barn late that afternoon with the draft team, Grace gathered the girls and they met him by the chicken coop. Seeing them, Peter pulled the team up short, lifted his hat from his head, and swept a hand across his sweat-streaked brow. His jaw tight, he glanced from them to the barn and back again.

"Everything all right?"

"Mother and foal are doing fine," Grace hastened to assure him. "I was just…" She cleared her throat and tried again. "There's a casserole in the oven. Stove is already off. The girls will want to spend time in the barn with the new foal, so if it's not a problem, as soon as the chickens are tended, I'll head home."

Under the weight of his attention, Grace concentrated on watching the hens scratch in the chicken run, as if she might see them find the source of salvation in the rocky soil.

"Are you all right?" This question was softer.

Pasting a smile on her face and widening her eyes to ensure no calfishness crept into them,

Grace met his gaze. "Oh, *ja*. Just have some things to do at home this evening." Like put together a puzzle that's already been done several times before. Or rearrange the limited cupboards that her tiny kitchen contained.

Peter nodded slowly before tipping his head toward where Malinda and Fannie, at the mention of the foal, were already racing for the barn. "Is this…working out for you?"

Glad of an excuse to look away, Grace watched the girls work together to swing open the big door. "Oh, *ja*. They are *wunderbar kinner*. They are no problem."

She looked back to see his jaw shift as he absorbed who the problem might be. Peter frowned as he ran his fingers through his short beard. "Do you want me to harness your mare?"

"*Nee*. I'll take care of it as soon as we, well, I—" her smile flickered at the absent girls "— tend to the chickens."

"I'll see you tomorrow then." With a last searching look, Peter's quiet word to the team set them into motion, and accompanied by a rattle of harness, they drew away.

Grace blew out a breath through pursed lips. Responsible and Mature. She'd managed one day. How many days was it until school started again and she could gracefully leave?

Whatever the number, it was too many.

* * *

Eighty-five days, not counting Sundays, Grace calculated on the way home. Surely she could be responsible and mature for eighty-five days. She'd managed to make it through a full school year with prankster James Yoder, who thankfully wouldn't return in the fall as he'd finished eighth grade, his final year of school.

Perhaps even before then, Lydia would be feeling better and the girls could return to her house? For some reason, dejection instead of relief churned in Grace's stomach at that possibility. She did enjoy the girls. And she never liked to leave a job unfinished.

Horse chores completed, she mounted the shallow steps to the back door of the home she was provided, along with the transportation and a small stipend, from the school district. Her shoulders wilted as she pondered the lengthy, and solitary, evening ahead. With a sigh, she opened the door and stepped inside, only to squeak as her bare foot landed in a puddle.

She jerked it back, trailing a splash of water onto the step. Her horrified gaze swept the interior of the small back porch, which opened into an equally small kitchen. It wasn't just a puddle. Water pooled over the house's worn squares of linoleum for as far as she could see.

Chapter Seven

Grace slumped against the porch door and stretched out her fingers—cramped from wringing out the mop more times than she cared to count—before pressing them against her aching back. Her head jerked up at the rattle of a buggy coming up the lane. Was help coming? Her eyes prickled, threatening tears. She bit her lower lip to ward them off. She'd been mopping for an hour and didn't seem to be making any progress on the lake inside her house.

Mop in hand, she descended the short steps and went to meet the rig as the Standardbred stopped at the faded wooden hitching post.

"That's quite the greeting." Youngster in her arms, Miriam Raber climbed down from the buggy before Aaron could make it around the vehicle to help. "Or should we take it as some kind of warning?"

"I'm afraid it's a warning." Grace's voice wobbled. She sniffed as she tilted her head toward the house. "It's a mess in there. I don't know what's happening. There's water all over the floor, and I can't seem to make it stop."

With a quick glance at his wife, Aaron strode up the shallow pavers that led to the back door and disappeared inside.

Miriam handed the toddler to Grace and took the mop handle from her stiff fingers. "Here. You look like you need a break. We stopped on our way into town to check on how your new job was going. *Gut* thing we did, so we can help you clean up your swamp."

Aaron reappeared in the doorway before they reached it. "It's your water heater. It's rusted out. I've turned off the water supply to it, as well as the gas. Being Amish benefited you, as it wasn't an electric heater." He grimaced. "Electricity and water don't mix."

Grace cuddled the little one closer, drawing comfort from his warm weight. "Well, at least I'll be all right once I get the water cleaned up then. I don't need the heater for hot water. Whenever I need some, I can warm it up on the stove."

Aaron's slow head shake didn't bode well for her. "I'm afraid lack of hot water is the least of the situation." He pointed to the drywall that flanked both sides of the water heater's corner placement. As she splashed across the wet floor to inspect it, Grace's jaw sagged at the sight of the wall's discolored and swollen surfaces.

"Oh no! I hadn't noticed. I'm so sorry." Her chin quivered. She was responsible for this destruction. She'd failed her school board landlords. "They're going to be so upset with me."

"Grace." Aaron's calming voice drew her attention. "These things happen. Appliances break down. The board knows that. Unless you kicked the water heater every day on your way through the porch?" At her vigorous head shake, he continued. "It's not your fault. You're on a well with hard water. Hard water can rust things. You don't have a water softener. This appliance is older than I am. It lasted a good long time."

Aaron rubbed a hand over his mouth as he considered the water heater. "But unfortunately, it's been leaking for some of that time. Which affected not only the wall, but also—" Aaron squatted and, with a calloused finger, flipped over one of the worn squares of tile to reveal the sodden subfloor "—this will have to be replaced. Depending, once we remove this, on the state of the floor below it, maybe that as well. With the potential for mold and—" he pushed on a section of flooring that gave under his fingers "—the possibility of falling through, you shouldn't stay here until it's fixed."

The toddler in her arms pushed back to regard her with rounded eyes when Grace moaned. "I should have noticed, but I didn't get home until after dark last night."

"It's been leaking for longer than that," Aaron reassured her. "It's not your fault."

Miriam straightened from where she'd been mopping and propped a hand on her hip. "Peter made you work that long on your first day?"

"*Nee*, we went fishing and had a picnic. Time got away from us. The fish were biting, the girls were laughing. It was…" her lips tipped up in a soft smile at the memory "…fun."

Miriam cocked her head and arched her eyebrow. She and Aaron shared a look. "Peter Lehman had fun?"

Aaron shook his head at his wife. "*Nee*, Miriam. Don't even think about it."

"*Ach*, I can think about it, Aaron."

"All right. You think about it. But don't act on it."

Miriam turned back to Grace. "We'll help you get the worst of it cleaned up here. Then you gather your things while we find a place for you to stay while this gets fixed."

Grace hesitated. Miriam was just trying to be helpful, but Grace felt like she was being swept along, much like the water they were mopping up. "I don't want to put you, or anyone else out."

"That's all right. I'm sure we'll find a satisfactory solution." Miriam gently patted her husband's scowling cheek as she passed him on her way to wring out the mop.

The worst of it, Grace discovered later, was not the water all over the floor of the little house, nor the guilt she felt for not having caught the situation before it became such a problem. The worst of it, she discovered while hanging towels on the clothesline that she'd used to finish wiping up the mess, was when a buggy rolled up the lane to reveal a grim-faced Peter. Malinda and Fannie leaned across him to poke their heads out the door.

Clipping on the last towel, Grace's fingers curled around the cool wire as Peter jumped down from the buggy.

"Get whatever you need from the house. You're coming home to stay with us." His voice was as remote as his expression.

"*Denki.* But that's not proper. I couldn't stay with you."

"*Ja,* you could. I'll move out to the *daadi haus.* It's not like I haven't lived there before. If it was far enough away for my—" Peter's jaw flexed "—wife, it should be far enough away for you. From what Aaron said, the floor has enough damage that it'll need extensive repair. And with most of the men in the fields right now, they won't be able to get to it right away."

The girls piled out of the buggy and trotted over to where Grace stood rooted by the clothesline. Fannie reached up to tug on Grace's apron. "Are you coming home with us?"

"Ah… I'm not sure." Seemingly satisfied with the answer, Fannie and Malinda darted away to explore more of the yard. Grace fixed her gaze on Peter and his gritted jaw. "I suppose Aaron and Miriam stopped by your place?"

"Why do you think I'm here? Miriam is like an eight-horse hitch. She'd run over about anything." His eyes narrowed on Grace. "Did you put her up to it?"

Grace let go of the clothesline to slap her arms over her chest at the accusation. "Oh no. I'd stay here if possible."

With a scowl, Peter marched past her and up the shallow steps into the house. The door banged behind him. A few minutes later he reappeared. "Well, it's not possible. So get your things so we can get home before it gets much later. We've got some work to do there to get you…settled. At least the surface water is mopped up. I'll come back tomorrow and pull up the tiles so we have a better idea of the subflooring situation."

His jutted jaw and the work-roughened hands propped on his lean hips insinuated that he had better things to do than fix her issues. It had been a lousy evening. Grace's body ached from hours of mopping. Though Aaron had claimed it wasn't her fault, guilt weighed heavy on her mind. What little space was left over was consumed with worry over where she'd stay and how long she'd be there.

Her exhaustion was ready tinder for the spark of anger that flared at being treated like unwanted baggage. She could either be angry or burst into tears. Which Grace wasn't going to do in front of him. "I can pull up my own tiles." Mimicking his position, she stabbed her fists onto her own hips while she glared at Peter.

This was the man I recently swooned over? That I considered warm and sensitive? He's about as warm and sensitive as a rabid badger.

"No, you can't. You were hired to do other things." Peter looked pointedly to where the girls were exploring her yard. "The members of the school district help take care of the district's needs. Malinda will be in school this fall. I can pull my own weight. It's only fair that I contribute. And the sooner the tiles are pulled and the subfloor checked, the sooner they can arrange for materials and labor to repair it."

"So, in other words, it's worth sacrificing time in the field tomorrow so you can get rid of me faster." Peter's jaw flexed. A wistful pang flickered through Grace when he didn't deny it. Suddenly weary, she bent to pick up the small clothes basket at her feet. "You might as well go back and get started on what you need to do tonight at your house for your *unwelcome* company. I'm not riding back with you."

Peter left the doorway to stalk across the yard. She hissed in a breath when he stopped in front of her. "And why not?"

"Because, unless you can drive two at one time, or plan to drive back and forth to feed the mare here, I need to bring my own horse and buggy."

For a moment, Grace thought she saw Peter's lips twitch. She scowled. Surely she was mistaken.

Pivoting, he headed for the small shed that housed the mare. "I'll harness her while you collect whatever things you need from the house," he tossed over his shoulder.

"For how long?" she called after him.

Peter turned so he was walking backward. His shoulders lifted in a sigh. "A few days. We can always come back for more if needed."

The girls came skipping back from their explorations. "Can we ride home with Grace?" piped Fannie.

Peter frowned, but his gaze locked with Grace's. "It's up to you."

"Of course. I'd love—" her eyes narrowed at their father before bending to address the girls as she took their hands "—*your* company."

* * *

Peter urged Hazel into a faster trot. The empty buggy seat beside him seemed immense in the girls' absence. But he couldn't blame them for wanting to ride home with Grace. He scrubbed a hand over the back of his neck. They'd be *gut* company for her. He'd been…unsettled at how much it'd bothered him to see her woebegone figure when they'd pulled into the yard. His immediate impulse had been to launch from the buggy, wrap his arms about her and assure her it would be all right. Thankfully, he'd stopped himself. Because it might never be all right again. The flooded little house, for sure and certain, would eventually be all right. But would he, with her now staying overnight in his home?

So he'd protected himself—a common response now regarding women—with anger. Grace had almost startled him out of his refuge when she'd fluffed up like a spitting kitten, back arched, with her enchanting version of a threatening yowl. If she'd had a tail, it would've stood straight up. He'd almost snickered, cracking his carefully erected defenses.

Peter jerked his hat down on his forehead, feeling the worn straw give under his fingers. Was this some form of punishment from *Gott*? Not only did he have to battle temptation during meals, which he'd determined to keep as short as possible, but now his evenings too? He couldn't expect Grace to retire at the same time the girls did, could he? And if she didn't, he'd be alone with her. Alone in the quiet house as it settled for the night. Alone with Grace in the soft lamplight. Alone…and tempted.

He wasn't concerned about physical temptation. After years of distaste regarding his wayward wife, he'd learned to stifle that. But was he strong enough to battle against the longing for companionship? The longing for the relationship he'd always envisioned? A partnership. One of mutual respect. Mutual admiration. Teamwork. Support. Love?

Peter pressed his hand against his chest. He was very much afraid he wasn't.

He turned Hazel into his lane as the sun dipped over the horizon. *Nee*, Grace might not retire when the girls did, but he could. He *would*. Peter sighed. To the *daadi haus* again. This time, not because he wanted to get away from a woman, but because he didn't.

Chapter Eight

Grace sighed as she listened to the *clip-clop* of Hazel's hooves trotting along the blacktop. The sound and the gentle motion of the buggy had lulled Fannie to sleep shortly after they left the house. The little girl's head lay on Grace's lap while Malinda, whose head was lolling on Grace's shoulder, looked to be dropping off soon as well.

Grace's attention wandered over the passing fields, visible through the drizzle on the buggy's storm front. She was glad the two little ones took up the center of the leather seat, pushing her to the edge and far away from their *daed*, whose rigid profile she'd been avoiding on this group trip into town.

Peter surely noted her pointed avoidance. Just as she noted his pointed departures from a room—from the whole house for that matter— the moment the girls went to bed. Having stayed the past few nights at Peter's farm, Grace had discovered long solitary evenings in an occupied large house could be as equally lonely as those in a little solo one. Maybe even more so. Why had she followed Miriam's lead, not once but twice, into this situation? Didn't she have a mind of her own?

"How much time do you need at the Piggly Wiggly to get your groceries?"

She raised an eyebrow. The question contained as many words as Peter had spoken to her since she'd arrived after dark two evenings ago. He'd met her at the buggy to carry in Malinda and Fannie, who had fallen asleep on the way over. Grace had brought in her things into one of the spare rooms while Peter had put the girls to bed. He'd passed her with a nod on the way to take care of her mare. He never returned to the big house.

At least his attitude had doused her foolish infatuation.

"Maybe thirty minutes. How long do you need for your errands?"

"It might take me a little longer. I told Isaiah Zook that I'd stop by the building supply store and tell them the measurements from where I'd pulled up the linoleum tiles from yesterday. As president of the school board, he'll order the replacement supplies and arrange for the repairs."

Grace wrinkled her nose at the reminder. She still felt discomfited regarding the damage. Almost as discomfited as she felt regarding her current living arrangements. At least it had rained yesterday, so she hadn't felt guilty that pulling up the tiles had kept Peter from fieldwork. Still, she hunched a shoulder and muttered, "The sooner, the better," to the passing countryside.

The seat creaked as Peter shifted. She could feel the weight of his gaze on the back of her *kapp*.

"For sure and certain."

He'd heard her mutter. Grace's face heated and her stomach dipped at his words. Even though she considered herself an intruder in his home, it was mortifying that he considered her one as well. Otherwise, why would he disappear every night, as if escaping from her? She had no one but herself to blame for being in this situation. She liked to please others, truly she did. But was she a weakling for constantly bending her will to go along with them? Her history seemed to indicate as much. For sure, their culture encouraged *gelassenheit*, yielding oneself to a higher authority. But at what point did she reserve any authority over her *own* life?

Grimacing, Grace narrowed her gaze on a distant speck on the blacktop. Anything to avoid the other adult occupant of the buggy. The speck grew as the distance between it, and their buggy diminished until she could make out a pony and cart, closing in on them at a rapid clip. Recognizing the outfit as it approached, Grace pressed a hand against the dashboard.

"Stop the buggy."

Peter whipped his head toward her at the abrupt directive.

"Stop the buggy. Please." Grace returned her attention to the pony as she braced herself. For what? She wasn't entirely sure.

Peter frowned and looked behind them to ensure no one was coming before slowing the buggy and directing it to the side of the road. Fannie lifted her head from Grace's lap at the change in movement. Malinda had straightened when the shoulder she'd been leaning against stiffened. The buggy rolled to a stop.

"What are you doing?" Peter's call followed Grace as she jumped down.

I wish I knew. But I feel like I'm a little wooden boat bouncing along in a flooded stream, doing everyone's will but my own. I'm even reluctant to go home, afraid I'll fall in with my mother's plans again. I'm capable of making a decision on my own. Aren't I? Heart thudding, Grace stopped at the center of the blacktop in the misty drizzle and waved a hand to flag down the pony cart and its passenger.

"*Guder mariye*, James," she greeted the passenger when the pony skidded to a stop on the damp pavement. The little golden mare's nostrils flared as she sucked in air. "Hello, Sunny," Grace acknowledged the pony with a stroke down her slick neck.

"Good morning to you, Miss Kauffman." The young teenaged boy wore a surprised smile as he stood up in the old cart. He glanced at the buggy parked along the side of the otherwise empty blacktop and echoed Peter. "What are you doing standing in the middle of the road? In the rain?"

Put like that, her abrupt action was more than a little foolish. Grace's cheeks flushed at the spectacle she was making of herself. She continued to pet the pony as the mare regained her breath. The action soothed them both. Grace drew in a gusty inhalation in sync with Sunny.

"Where are you going in such a hurry, James?"

"I'm heading home. I've been fishing." The boy jerked a thumb to the fishing pole beside him on the cart. "At least until it started to rain."

Grace had been glad James Yoder was one of the boys who had finished eighth grade, and therefore school, this year. It wasn't that he was a mean-spirited boy. Quite the opposite, in fact. He always wore a smile. An engaging, infectious one. It was just that whenever there'd been pranks—crickets on the girls' *kapps*, frogs dropped into the latrines, the incident with the chalkboard erasers when Grace feared she'd never get them clean again—James was always the instigator or executor.

None of his younger siblings in school, and there were several of them, gave her issues, for which Grace was extremely grateful. But the one thing she would miss about James when school started up next year was his pony, Sunny.

Grace had made a friend of the golden mare during recesses when she wasn't recruited to umpire a baseball game. The hitching posts afforded Grace a good view of the school yard. She'd visit the animals while she kept an eye on the children's activities. She'd been drawn to Sunny, who reminded her of a favorite pony she'd had as a little girl. Grace had assumed Sunny would return in the fall with the younger Yoder children until one of James's brothers set her straight. An uncle had given James the pony years ago, and Sunny was his and his alone.

The news had dismayed Grace. It wasn't that James abused the pony. It was just that Sunny was getting some age on her. While her energy might've matched James's when they were younger, as they'd both grown older, those levels had diverged.

Grace worried her lower lip as she contemplated the pony and its master. "Looks like you've grown even in the short time since school has ended, James. I can easily believe that in a few short years, you'll be sixteen and ready to enter your *rumspringa*."

James straightened his shoulders at her comment. "*Ja*, Miss Kauffman."

"You'll be ready for your own horse and buggy, perhaps one outfitted a little differently than that one." She tipped her head toward Peter's rig, with its family-oriented interior as opposed to anything a teenaged boy would desire.

James's face fell. "My *daed* has said with sixteen *kinner*, he couldn't buy one for all of us, so he won't buy one for any of us. And with no job, I won't be able to afford a buggy."

What am I doing? Everyone would think I'm being foolish. For a moment, Grace reconsidered. She drew in a deep breath. *I am capable of making a decision on my own.* Clearing her throat, she gently combed her fingers through the pony's blond forelock. "Um, if you sold Sunny, that would start a little nest egg for you."

James frowned. "How would I get around then?"

Grace picked a few burrs from the pony's mane. "I imagine you could buy a scooter, particularly a used one, for a fraction of her cost. Fewer chores to do with that as well."

James lifted his obviously handed-down hat and scratched his head. "I hadn't really thought about it." He considered the pony before him.

"But it might be a *gut* idea. I'll mention it to my *daed*, he talks to a lot of folks. He might know who'd be interested in a pony."

Grace's heart was pounding such that she could feel the pulse beating at her throat. *This is a foolish, foolish idea.* Still, the words were out before she could stop them. "I'd buy her from you."

"You?" James' outburst was quickly followed by his lowered brow. "How much would you pay?" The cart creaked as he stepped down from it and came to stand on the other side of the pony's head. He began to pet the mare as well. Above his affable smile, he studied Grace. It was obvious behind his narrowed gaze that James was running more calculations in his head than he'd ever done during any of the math classes she'd taught him.

Grace swallowed hard and named a sum that was a good share of her savings. Her fingers twisted in Sunny's mane. She didn't know if the amount would earn her a pony, or a laugh.

James tugged on his ear as his gaze dropped to the mare between them. Grace held her breath.

"I suppose I could let her go for that."

Grace's fingers tightened on the pony's mane as her knees wobbled. Her heart continued to pound as *I did it* collided immediately with *what have I done?*

"You want to buy the cart too?"

She almost rolled her eyes at the question. She could hardly afford the pony. "Thanks, but no."

"*Gut* thing, as it's my older brother's."

Guilt prompted her to make the offer, though now the transaction had been agreed upon, she hoped it wouldn't be accepted. "As you've made the decision to sell her, do you want to consider selling her to one of your siblings?"

James shook his head. "Nah. They'd rather borrow her than buy her. And I think you'd give her a *gut* home, Miss Kauffman. She likes you. She's been a *gut* pony. I'd like to know she's happy."

Grace's nose prickled with threatening tears. At least they wouldn't be noticeable with the sporadic raindrops dotting her face. "I'll try to make her so."

James adjusted the bridle around the mare's ears. "You want to take her now?"

"*Nee.* I can wait. You need to get your brother's cart home. Besides, I don't have the money on me now. You just bring her over when you're ready and I'll pay you."

The arrangement seemed to satisfy the boy as he nodded and returned to climb into the cart.

"And James?"

He looked up as he gathered the reins. "*Ja,* Miss Kauffman?"

"Don't run my pony so hard."

He grinned lopsidedly before shrugging. "*Ja*, Miss Kauffman."

Grace stepped back. Sunny's hoofs tapped on the blacktop as James directed the mare around her and headed off at a sedate pace. Several yards down the road, he glanced back at Peter, visible through the buggy's storm front, and called over his shoulder, "Bring her over where?"

Grace didn't have an answer. Trembling from her impulsive and foolish action, she crossed her arms over her chest. She hurried toward the buggy, only to stop when Peter's quiet query reached her.

"*Ja*, Miss Kauffman. Bring her over where? You have room in your little shed for a pony in addition to your Standardbred?"

Raindrops tapped on the roof overhead. Peter winced when his wry comment caused Grace to pause on the blacktop before she climbed into the buggy with her rain-splotched dress and dampened cheeks.

He should be angered. She'd manipulated the boy. Dangling the prospect of transportation that boys his age would aspire to as they approached their *rumspringa* and the liberties that accompanied it.

Surprisingly, as he took in the tendrils that curled free of her *kapp* and her earnest and shaken expression as she rubbed at her damp sleeves, he wasn't. Instead, admiration flooded him regarding her concern for the pony. Although they might've been a good fit once, the boy had outgrown the animal. And instead of chastising the youth, she'd allowed him some pride, and a more than reasonable price for the little mare.

Peter reached into the back bench for the blanket he kept there. He handed it to the shivering woman. After a brief hesitation, she took it and wrapped it around her shoulders.

"You always leap before you look?"

She used a corner of the blanket to blot some rain from her face. "Sometimes. But I'm glad I did this." Her words were quiet, but fierce nonetheless.

After checking for traffic, Peter directed Hazel back onto the road.

"Did you just buy a pony?" Undeterred by the damp skirt, Fannie scrambled onto Grace's lap.

Grace settled the girl more comfortably for the both of them. "I guess I did."

"Is it coming to our house like your mare did? Is she going to stay in our barn with Tanner and Bella?"

"I…uh…"

Grace darted a look at Peter. He rubbed a hand across his mouth to hide his smile. She wasn't so fierce now. Keeping his attention on the road ahead and his face impassive, he spoke into the void. "I suppose Tanner wouldn't mind the company. In fact, he might enjoy seeing someone else in the barn around his size."

Peter was jolted by the joy that lit Grace's eyes. "*Denki*," she mouthed, and her gaze softened. On him. His heart lurched and his mouth went dry as he held her gaze.

To his relief, she dropped her attention to focus on straightening out the pleats in the back of Fannie's *kapp*. "You could take the cost of boarding it out of my wages."

Peter took a moment to recover, camouflaging a hard swallow with a grunt. "I don't pay you enough for there to be much to deduct. I don't think what feed this pony will eat would break me. And I have extra stalls available, especially since Lu—" he caught himself. "I have the stall space." Peter's hands tightened on the reins as he stared out over the dash. He'd needed the reminder. Needed to remember that he had—*has* a wife and, as such, had no business being mesmerized by the joy that frequently lit this woman. Joy, other than the girls, was not a part of his life. Lucetta's dark shadow, even in her absence, loomed endlessly into his future.

"We can keep it until Grace's home is fixed and she returns to it. Which can't be soon enough."

Grace stiffened at his brusque words. She stared out the storm front as well.

Peter bit down hard on the inside of his cheek to keep from reaching for her hand. To keep from apologizing. But the words and tone had been necessary. Necessary to rebuild the barricade that tumbled down brick by brick at each one of her smiles, her soft glances, her cheerfulness. Bricks he desperately needed to shore up again.

The remainder of the journey to the Piggly Wiggly was filled with the girls' questions regarding the pony, which Grace patiently answered. Peter didn't speak again.

He'd been looking for reasons to warn other men about Grace, as he'd learned women were not to be trusted. But with Grace…he was beginning to wonder. Peter purposely turned his mind to calculating the number of new tiles and other supplies needed to repair her house's damaged floor. He'd speak with Isaiah about how soon men could be free to do so. He was desperately afraid any protective wall he built against this woman wouldn't last long.

Chapter Nine

Grace knitted the last stitch on the row and lowered her needles to her lap. She smiled as her gaze dropped to where the girls were busy with the colors and coloring books she'd picked up at the Pig. Though she didn't look at him, she was aware of every move Peter made from his chair on the far side of the common room. A creak of the ottoman advised he'd crossed or uncrossed his ankles. A rattled paper announced a turned page of the *Budget*.

Rattled. An appropriate word for her and her feelings toward Peter as his demeanor galloped from winter to summer and back again like a runaway horse. One moment, he was silent and reserved, tempting her to poke him to get a reaction or to harness her mare, drive back to her little house and take the risk of falling through the floor. The next moment, his slow smile and the glint in his eyes would send her stomach fluttering like all the butterflies in Wisconsin were trapped inside.

Yesterday, from shortly after she'd bought the pony—the deed still amazed and delighted her—until Peter had disappeared into the *daadi haus*, winter had blown through. This morning, a summer breeze stirred to warm her when she'd entered the barn to retrieve the egg baskets and discovered he'd already prepared a stall for Sunny's arrival.

The butterflies had taken flight to remain aloft throughout lunch and dinner, fluttering to new heights whenever her gaze had collided with his or their hands had brushed while passing plates. The foolish insects showed no sign of settling down after supper when the household retired together to the common room, like it was natural. Like they were…a family.

Except they weren't. And she needed to remember that. It was difficult to do so.

When Peter was in winter, he was a handsome man. A responsible, hardworking, intelligent man. A wonderful father. All admirable qualities. But when he was in summer… Grace quietly hissed in a breath as the butterflies in her stomach launched into frantic acrobatics. In summer, he was kind. Dryly funny. Caring. Respectful. Yet it was the hint of vulnerability that made her want to help shoulder his burdens, to curve gentle hands around the strong column of his neck and pull his head down to bestow a reassuring kiss.

Grace's cheeks flamed as she scowled at the project in her lap. She'd dropped a stitch. No surprise when her mind had been far from knitting and purling. With a sigh, she gathered up her needles and began picking out the last row.

What if Peter's winter demeanor didn't chase her away anymore? What if she discounted it and only saw the summer one? These butterflies were different from the schoolgirl giddiness she'd experienced several mornings ago. These included an ache for Peter when he was in winter. An ache to resurrect his slow smile when he retreated into stoic silence. An ache to smooth the lines of worry from his brow when he thought no one was looking.

The light dimmed, casting shadows into the room. Grace glanced out the window toward where clouds billowed, blocking the sun as it sank on the horizon. In the dwindling light, she finished tearing out the row without finding the missing stitch. She grimaced. No surprise. Her mind wasn't on the yarn, but on Peter. Would he disappear, as was his habit, as soon as the girls went to bed tonight? What would she do if he didn't? The butterflies darted about.

"Time to brush your teeth and wash up for bed, girls." To their credit, Malinda and Fannie didn't groan at her words. They gathered up their colors and books and put them away before plodding to the bathroom.

"And don't forget to wash your feet and legs. We worked in the garden today, and I don't want to find all the dirt from there has been transferred to your bedroom by your bare feet," Grace called after them.

The sitting room was suddenly empty. And quiet. The rattle of Peter's newspaper sounded like a thunder clap.

"How many younger siblings do you have?"

She jumped at his question. Setting her knitting aside, she looked up to find his amused gaze on her. "Several. You can tell?"

His mouth tilted in a half smile. "*Ja.* You're *gut* with children."

"That's nice to know, as someday I hope to have some of my own."

He held her gaze a moment before nodding. He rarely asked personal questions. Did this mean she could ask one as well? Before he could return his attention to his paper, she blurted, "How about you?"

An odd expression crossed his face. "I already have some of my own."

Grace rolled her eyes. "I mean siblings."

"Those too."

The thuds of little feet on linoleum preceded

the return of the girls. Reaching Grace, they lifted their legs for her inspection.

"Nice." Grace nodded approvingly before gently turning Malinda around and unpinning the *kapp* from her dark hair. "Hmm. I think you need to make a return trip and wash behind your ears. I could grow radishes in what you still have back there."

"How about my ears?" Fannie tipped her head closer, bumping Grace's elbow.

Grace made an exaggerated check behind the little girl's ears as she unpinned her *kapp* as well. "I think I could even grow turnips behind yours." She gave a gentle pat to Fannie's backside. "Off you go again."

Fannie and Malinda giggled as they trotted back to the bathroom. Peter watched them go, a smile on his face.

"Do any of them live around here?"

He blinked a moment, as if trying to recall the topic before shaking his head. "Siblings? *Nee.* They're all back in Kentucky."

Grace frowned sympathetically. "That's a ways. Do you ever get to visit? Do they come up here, or you and the girls go down there?"

Again, a shake of his head. "*Nee.* Not really." It was quiet for a moment. Grace figured that was the end of the conversation, until he cleared his throat. "How about you? Your family ever come up from Iowa since you've been here?"

"No." Grace wrinkled her nose. "And I'm not sure I want them to right now."

His eyebrows rose. "Sounds like there's a story there."

At the patter of the girls' footfalls, she smiled. "It's one that will have to wait." She stood as Fannie and Malinda burst into the room and rushed over for reinspection. "All clean." Grace approved their obviously vigorous efforts.

"Can I pick out the book?"

"That sounds fair, Malinda, as Fannie chose the one last night." Grace didn't know how she'd taken over the bedtime rituals, but she had, from the second night she'd stayed. She didn't know what they'd been before, but the girls seemed satisfied with the new arrangement, and Peter hadn't argued. She picked up the lantern by her chair for the trip upstairs.

The girls took turns leaning against the wooden arm of Peter's chair as they kissed him goodnight. Grace pressed a hand against the energized butterflies in her stomach as she watched them stand on tiptoe to do so.

What would it be like to rest my hand on that sturdy shoulder? To lean in and press my lips against his cheek? What would he do if I did so?

Grace's eyes widened and she flushed again

at her renegade thoughts. Her blush turned crimson when Peter looked up while Fannie bussed his cheek to catch her considering gaze on him. Grace jerked the lantern to arm's length, hoping the shadows would veil her expression. Could he tell she was dreaming of kissing him goodnight as well?

She retreated to the narrow stairway, the girls following in her wake. They didn't take long to settle into bed. Even so, when Grace crept softly back down, it was to find a glowing lantern in the otherwise empty room. Her shoulders sagged. She crossed to the lantern and turned it out before returning to her bedroom upstairs, her steps much heavier on the wooden stairs.

She loved the girls. There was no question about that. And their father? She shouldn't. Because no matter how much the situation might make it seem like they were a family, they weren't. And never would be. But her butterflies wouldn't listen. And neither would the ache in her heart.

Hours later, Grace jerked her head up from her pillow. Had that been a cry? Or just the rattle of windows shaken by the thunderclap? Pushing up onto her elbows, she focused everything on listening. Rain pelted against the side of the house, making it sound like an abundance of small rocks were being thrown against its broad sides. Wind whistled through nearby trees.

She held her breath. There it was again. Just as the echoes of thunder rolled away. A whimper. Followed by…a stifled sob? Grace tossed the covers back. Grabbing the small quilt from the bed, she flung it over her shoulders and hurried to the girls' bedroom.

Lightning flickered, briefly illuminating the room as she stepped through the doorway. Grace used the next flash to find the lamp she'd left in there earlier. Her fingers fumbled to light it as another muffled sob was almost drowned out by the accompanying burst of thunder. When she finally got the lamp lit and moved it to a small stand closer to the bed, its dim glow revealed the girls huddled in the center of the mattress, their eyes wide, the covers pulled up to their chins. With a squeak of the bedsprings, Grace joined them there before they could scramble to her. They quickly shifted to allow her to slip between them and wrap an arm around each.

"I don't like storms," Malinda whispered as she huddled closer.

"Me either." Fannie's voice ended in a squeak when thunder and lightning burst simultaneously overhead.

Grace opened her mouth to reassure them only to squeak herself when the next bolt illuminated a figure in the doorway. Her heart lurched into her throat at the dark shape. She shrank against the headboard as the girls scrambled onto her lap.

When the figure stepped far enough into the room to enter the lamp's glow, Malinda lurched from the bed.

"Daed!" She launched herself into his arms.

It took a moment for Grace to coax her heart back down from her throat. She adjusted the covers around herself and Fannie—who seemed content to take sole possession of her lap—as she stared at what the dim light revealed of Peter.

His feet were bare. She'd never dreamed of seeing his bare toes. They and his hatless, bowl-cut hair—tousled and obviously damp from his trip across the open porch in the weather—made him as vulnerable as she could have ever imagined him. That, along with the close-eyed expression on his shadowed face as he hugged his daughter, made her tumble over the edge. Grace shuddered, along with the house, on an overhead clap of thunder. The sound punctuated what she could no longer deny.

She loved him.

Peter's eyes opened to meet her stare as he rubbed Malinda's back. A moment later, he turned away to find the rocking chair in the corner where Grace had read books to the girls earlier. He eased himself into it and began to rock while the storm rumbled. The house groaned as another gust of wind buffeted it.

"Is the house going to blow away?" Malinda whimpered.

Fannie drew herself into a smaller knot on Grace's lap.

"Nee," Peter murmured. "The house is just sighing. Much like you sigh when you've been working or playing all day. It's saying, 'That's enough,' to the wind. 'It's been a long day and I'm tired of your howling. Why don't you just quiet down so we can all get some sleep?' And it will, eventually. This house has been here a long time."

Fannie flinched in Grace's lap as rain slapped against the siding. "Why does it have to do that?" She sniffled.

"Ach, Fannie. How could I grow my crops if there was never rain to water them? I can't haul that much water, can you?"

"But does it have to come this way, *Daed*? Why can't it just come down quietly instead, like it did the other day?"

"The weather has different moods. Just like you and your sister. Sometimes you play well together and sometimes not."

"I don't like this mood."

"Well—" Grace could hear the smile in Peter's voice "—we'll make it through, Malinda. Just like we do when those around us get into moods. We might not like them, but we make it through."

The three Lehmans were silent. Grace almost spoke into the void when she realized they were probably thinking about their life before their *mamm* had left.

"Do you think Tanner is all right?" Malinda pushed up from where she'd been leaning against his shoulder.

The storm had moved on enough that Grace could hear the creak of the rocker over the departing thunder.

"*Ja.* Tanner is in the barn with Bella. It's a sturdy barn, as is this house."

Grace's eyes had adjusted enough to the dim lighting that she could see Peter gently tap the end of his daughter's nose with his finger. "Tanner might be worried about you too. We'll go out and see him first thing in the morning so both of you can check on each other."

Malinda nodded solemnly. "That would be *gut.*"

Fannie yawned, the sound carried across the now quieter room.

Peter eased the rocker to a stop. "Morning will be here before you know it. Are you ready to rejoin your sister and get a little sleep tonight?"

At Malinda's nod, Peter rose lithely from the chair and carried her over to the bed, reaching it just as Grace climbed off the mattress. She stepped back as he settled Malinda upon it and adjusted the covers over both girls. When he tipped his head toward the door, she crept in that direction.

"Do you want the lamp on or off?"

It was quiet a moment as Malinda considered. Fannie was already an inert lump under the blankets. "Off. We'll be all right now. *Denki, Daed,*" she murmured before her head sank onto her pillow.

Peter turned out the lamp and joined Grace at the doorway, where he paused. When the girls didn't stir, he proceeded down the stairway. She quietly followed him. As they emerged into the common room, Peter turned to look at her. He hesitated a moment before continuing on to the door that led to the porch.

Grace curled her toes against the cool linoleum. She wanted to stop him, but to do so, with the way she was feeling, might be trouble.

"*Denki*, Peter." Did that whisper come from her? "I'm not sure I would've known what to say to comfort them."

Hand on the doorknob, Peter spoke to the wooden panels of the door. "You would've figured it out. As I said, you're *gut* with children."

"That may be, but I'm still glad you came in."

His shoulders lifted in a sigh. For the first

time, Grace noted that, instead of looping over his shoulders, his suspenders hung from the waist of his broadfall pants, evidence of his haste to reach his daughters.

Peter kept a hand on the doorknob as if it was an anchor. "I had thought, when I was staying in the *daadi haus*, which was most of my marriage, that Lucetta was surely comforting the girls during bad storms. After she'd left and I moved back into the house with them, I learned differently."

Grace didn't have to see his face to know his expression was bitter. "The girls are fortunate to have you. You're a *wunderbar* father."

Peter shook his head wearily. "Though it took me a while, that's the one thing I think I may be doing right." He finally turned to her, his gaze skimming over the small quilt slung over her shoulders and down her nightgowned figure before he locked eyes with her. He rubbed a hand over his mouth. "I have to keep trying to do what's right." He jerked the door open and stepped out into the night.

Grace pulled the quilt more tightly about her. Her stomach clenched at Peter's words. She should as well, but what was right? Staying distant and ignoring this family's obvious wounds? Or providing the support she longed to give? Even if that support included an impossible love?

Chapter Ten

"That row isn't straight."

To his surprise, Peter's shoulders didn't hitch, nor did his teeth grit, at the criticism. In fact, he smothered a smile at Malinda's assessment. A response he wouldn't have thought possible, even to a critique from a five-year-old, after years of being the recipient of Lucetta's relentless carping.

"*Ach*, you're right, Malinda. Glad you're keeping an eye on it. Anything worth doing is worth doing well." Indeed, the shallow furrow he'd been hoeing across the garden wasn't straight. Because, instead of ensuring he didn't bump the guiding line of twine that stretched across the smoothly tilled soil, his attention had constantly flickered to the woman dropping seeds into the next furrow over. A woman who, with her trim figure and golden hair swept neatly into her *kapp*, was easy on the eyes. A woman who, he'd been discovering, was easy on his soul. One he'd rarely, if at all, heard criticize. One he could… trust?

One who, against all his best efforts to the contrary, he'd already fallen in love with.

Peter closed his eyes and leaned on his hoe. He'd battled his feelings as best he could. But his foolishness wasn't a surprise. Anyone who feeds or bestows kindness on an abused dog or cat knows that animal will keep coming around unless it is shooed away.

But Grace didn't shoo. Instead, she was approachable, patient, encouraging, fun, charming. Peter swallowed as he recalled the storm a few nights ago. Enticing. Much too enticing. Now, instead of counting the days until her house was fixed, Peter treasured each day that a work party was not yet scheduled to do so. Treasured each evening she was in his home, even though he still went off to the *daadi haus* as soon as Malinda and Fannie went to bed. Treasured the hours after chores and before the lanterns were extinguished in the girls' room. Treasured the vision of a life he'd once dreamed of living.

Foolish, foolish man, Peter grimly chided himself as he returned to where the row deviated and hoed the furrow directly under the untouched twine, pausing every few feet to look up and check with a monitoring Malinda.

She solemnly bobbed her little chin in approval. "That's better, *Daed*. You're doing really *gut* now."

He lifted a hand in acknowledgment. He'd been chilled when he'd first heard the faultfinding in Malinda's pint-sized voice. Even though she was gone, was Lucetta's dark shadow going to linger over his girls? Was Malinda, either through nature or short, intense years of nurture, going to be like her mother? The prospect had made him ill.

But lately, his daughter's somber judgments were almost always followed with an encouragement. Peter flicked his gaze from his furrow to take in the slender feet and ankles working along the next one over. The one he credited with the change. The one who was easy on the eyes, easy on his soul and, of utmost importance, good with his children.

"*Denki*, Malinda. It must be your coaching."

Another nod from his daughter. "We'll put the peas in that row."

"I can help plant those too." Fannie piped up from where she was carefully smoothing soil, the consistency of coffee grounds, over the seeds Grace was planting.

"*Ja*. As soon as you help me finish this row of lettuce."

Peter looked up. His gaze collided with Grace's. He'd been doing that all too much lately. Sighing, he backtracked to scrape another layer of dirt into the previous foot of furrow. Charged with energy just from her smile, he'd dug it two inches deeper than necessary.

Foolish, foolish man. You galloped recklessly into what you thought was love once. Look how that turned out. Your love for this one, given the situation, is no better. In fact, it's considerably worse.

Peter kept his head down as he hoed. He was good at burying his feelings. Usually. His hands tightened on the hoe handle. But what of the girls? What if they got too attached to Grace? Got to loving her as he did? Caring for *Aendi* Lydia was one thing. She was family. Grace was not. She would not be staying in their lives.

But what if she did? Along with foolishly tumbling into love, an even more dangerous emotion was slowly taking root in him. He hadn't grasped what it was at first, as it kept fluttering just out of reach. But as he spent more time with Grace, he recognized it.

Hope. Hope for the future was seeping through hairline cracks in the protective wall he had built years ago. He needed to squelch it. Hope could be futile.

Having reached the end of the row, Peter squinted toward the sun, which was flirting with the horizon. "If we're going to finish before sunset, we need to move a little faster."

"All right. Fannie and I will do the peas and

you and Grace plant the tomatoes. And that should about finish it." Hands on miniature hips, Malinda surveyed the garden the females had been working in since he'd finished tilling it up.

Grace brushed the dirt from her hands as she straightened at the end of her row. "Sounds like we have our assignments." Her bare toe nudged one of the trays she and the girls had picked up from a local greenhouse earlier in the day. "Girls, how many tomatoes are we putting in?"

Fannie pointed a tiny finger at the trays with their rows of small, fragile plants. "One hundred!"

"One hundred? Are you sure? And are you going to eat that many tomatoes, Fannie?"

"You don't even like tomatoes, Fannie." Malinda scoffed as she studied the trays, her mouth moving silently as she counted the individual seedlings. "Twenty-four?"

"*Gut!* That's right. Enough to give us some for the table and some we can later use for canning."

Peter set the hoe down and crossed to the stake anchoring the twine. Tugging it free, he moved it to the portion of the garden reserved for the tomatoes and, eyeballing the distance to the next row over, pounded it into the ground. *Us. We.* What beautiful words. He braced himself against the warmth that infused him at their sound. Since his marriage, he'd only known those words in conjunction with his girls. His wife's words had been *I*. Or *you*, spoken derisively. Usually followed by *never* or *always*. Even now, his shoulders tensed fractionally at the memory.

Any tomato harvest was at least two to three months away. Would Grace still be here then? It was possible, if school hadn't started yet. But the way he felt, would it be dangerous to let her stay that long? He drew in a shaky breath.

After aligning the stake at the far end of the garden with its partner and getting another nod of approval from Malinda, he walked back across the plot to where Grace had relocated the trays by the first stake.

"It's summer and you're still teaching."

Grace grinned as she deftly popped a seedling with its small pod of soil from the tray. "I guess I am." She wrinkled her nose. "I never expected to teach. But I've found I really like it."

Peter didn't ask what she'd expected to do. Like most girls in the Amish community, the answer was to get married. He picked up the spade he'd brought earlier and moved the pail of water for the plants to the end of the row. His girls had informed him, even before Grace's first day, that she was looking for a beau. Peter clenched his jaw until it ached. Though she said *us* and *we*, those words were for someone else. They had to be.

He jabbed the spade into the ground and rocked

it back and forth before indicating to Grace to set the seedling along the back of the blade. She did so, holding it in place as she dipped a can of water from the pail and poured it into the plant's new home. Peter carefully withdrew the spade and stepped on the ground in front of the plant, wedging it in.

They moved down the row. Mundane work. Work they did well as a team. Peter treasured every moment of it as he gazed at Grace's slender neck and the top of her bent head.

"How are you doing over there, girls?" he called without looking in their direction.

"Gut, Daed!"

Peter froze when Grace looked up to catch him staring.

"James hasn't brought over Sunny yet. Do you think he's forgotten that I'm buying her?" She worried her lower lip. "Or changed his mind?"

Peter shook his head, glad to be able to latch on to a topic. Any topic. *"Nee.* As soon as it was dry enough after that rain, the Yoders have been harvesting their first hay cutting. With their cattle, they cut a lot. Most all the family is involved. Particularly the boys. I'm sure he's just been very busy with that lately."

Her expression relaxed. "That's a relief. I wondered if my trust, and judgment, had been misplaced."

"*Nee*, I think you're safe there. James is a *gut* boy. Probably just gets lost in the shuffle with all the other *kinner* in the household."

"That's good to know. I don't want to think I'm that wrong about someone."

Her smile warmed Peter more than the midday sun had when he'd been in the field earlier. It also chilled him. Chilled him because he wanted to respond to it. Chilled him because Grace's smile and the way her eyes sparkled said she had thoughts about *him*. Interested thoughts. Dangerous thoughts, as they were ones he shared.

He swallowed. Her cheeks flushed. Heat rose on his own face. Grace reached up to secure a tendril of hair that had escaped, leaving a streak of dirt on her otherwise pristine *kapp*. Peter longed to reach out and brush it away. Grace's smile turned shy. She broke eye contact, looking down to the plastic tray that crackled as she struggled to free another seedling. He could hear her clear her throat.

"I picked up the mail already. I put the *Budget* by your chair and the rest of the mail on the corner of your desk."

Peter remembered to breathe. He nodded even though she couldn't see him as she finally freed the plant. "*Denki*," he murmured.

That was another thing he wasn't used to. The thoughtful little things, like putting the newspaper next to where he'd be reading it. A smile curved his lips. The reaction had almost become natural. But the earlier chill still prickled up his spine. She was interested. He was interested. A combustible combination.

The chill consolidated into a cold ball in his stomach. His love, the emerging hope. It was wrong. But so, so tempting. Peter stabbed the spade into the soil again. "The girls look to be about done. We need to hurry up if we're going to finish before dark."

Peter picked up the stack of mail from the corner of his scarred desk. Flipping through the envelopes, he automatically sorted the advertisements from the bills, twisting his lips as he dropped the former, which he had no money to spend on, straight into the wastepaper basket, while placing the latter, which he hoped he had funds for, into the desk slot he'd allocated for that purpose. His fingers froze on the last envelope, one much thicker than the others. Tension gripped the back of his neck as he recognized the handwriting that scrawled his name and address across the front.

Lucetta's handwriting.

His attention darted to the blank return address. Where was she? Why was she writing after all these months? Was she coming back? He drew in shaky breaths as bile maliciously tickled the back of his throat. Slumping a hip against the edge of the desk, he slit the letter open. With a bracing inhalation, he unfolded the lined paper and scanned the contents. Upon reaching Lucetta's sprawling signature at the bottom of the third page, he read through the letter again before lifting his gaze to stare blankly across the room, crinkling the pages in his hand.

She was unhappy.

It wasn't a surprise. For Lucetta, happiness—if it existed—was only momentary. Only as long as someone did her will. Exactly as she wished it. Through manipulation or false charm on her part, as she didn't trust folks to oblige her out of goodwill of their own.

His lips tightened. Why *would* she think that, when she had no goodwill toward her fellow man herself? And why would she have expected to find that in the *Englisch* world when she didn't see it in the Amish community where *gelassenheit*—self-surrender, or giving oneself up to the will of *Gott* and others—was a tenet of their faith?

The *Englisch* man she'd disappeared with—the one she had thought worthy of leaving her husband, children, community and culture for—had abandoned her. Though she had a place to stay, she'd had to find work, something Lucetta was poorly acquainted with.

Nee, learning Lucetta was unhappy wasn't a surprise.

Learning of her pregnancy was.

Apparently, that was the reason for the *Englischer*'s departure. Peter closed his eyes and let his head droop until his chin rested on his chest as he mentally calculated the number of months Lucetta had been gone. He didn't know how far along she was, but, even should Lucetta try to claim it as such, there was no possible way the *boppeli* was his.

His wife was having another man's child. The knowledge twisted in his gut like a dull knife. Had that been Lucetta's intent in sending the letter? To hurt him? With her, it was hard to tell. And what did it say about him that his wife would rather have another man's child than his own? That she would rather have another man? That, from the outset of their marriage, she made sure he knew he wasn't enough? Made sure anyone who would listen knew it as well.

Peter's head swam. Papers crackled beneath his palms as he braced his hands on the desk. He opened his eyes, panting until the room stopped whirling. When his legs felt solid again, he straightened.

He'd been thinking about himself. What about the poor child? Its father had already deserted it. And its *mamm*… Lucetta had a hard time caring for anyone but herself. It was something that had always confounded him. How could someone raised in their society, one that considered the whole of the community as much more than the individual, even down to their homogenous dress and hair styles, be so selfish? Did not the *Biewel* say to not be vain? To think not just of oneself but others? To even think of others better than themselves? He was far from perfect on the practice himself, but at least he tried.

He meticulously smoothed out the crinkled papers. He didn't need to read the letter again to understand its underlying message. Whatever allure the *Englisch* world had held for Lucetta, it had faded.

She didn't specifically state that she wanted to come back, but she was thinking it. Peter glanced again at the envelope. No return address on it or the letter. There would be more letters in the future. Ones that would specifically outline what she wanted from him.

He sagged into the worn desk chair, the old wheels creaking as they scooted slightly under his weight.

Would he need to go get her, or would she just show up at the farm? He grimaced at the possibility. And for how long? Even if Lucetta should stay, due to her departure after baptism, she'd been excommunicated from the church. While they already hadn't shared a bedroom for a long while, under the *bann*, he couldn't even eat from the same table as her. He couldn't take anything from her hand. Nor could anyone else in the community.

His sister-in-law Lydia had faced shunning. But even prior to her kneeling confession in front of the church, she'd already returned a changed woman. Excommunication was intended for correcting sins. Though Lucetta's were grievous, should she sincerely confess and repent, she could be welcomed back into the fold. The trouble with Lucetta... Peter shook his head; he didn't know if she had ever been sincere. About anything. How long would any "repentance" of hers last? If it did, would he grow to love her? He tensed at the thought. Had he ever?

Bile coated the back of Peter's throat. His future lay before him like a bottomless pit. He'd expected trials in his life, but not that his would be like Hosea of the *Biewel*, with his promiscuous wife Gomer, whom *Gott* had said to marry and keep taking back even when she ran off with other men.

Gott hadn't told him to marry Lucetta. *Gott* had probably even sent warnings against doing so through the advice of others. Advice he hadn't heeded. Peter exhaled until it felt like all the breath he'd ever breathed had left his body.

Of course he would take her back. She was his wife.

He scrubbed his hands over his face. What would Lucetta's return do to the girls? They had been doing so well with Grace.

Oh, Grace. Peter's fingers curled into his hair, and he tugged hard on the strands. *How foolish of me to have hoped for any kind of future aside from what I have. I am trapped in this marriage. One so different from what I'd dreamed of. But this is my lot. There's no escape.*

His hands dropped to his lap. No escape in his world. If he divorced Lucetta, he'd be shunned as well. He stared at his hands, calloused from hard work. He could find work and support himself and a family in the *Englisch* world. The *Englisch* world, where he could get a divorce. Where he could be free from Lucetta. If he allowed himself to do so.

Peter curled his hands into fists. *Nee*, he'd made a commitment before *Gott*. No matter the culture he lived in. Besides, to leave would be to lose the support of a culture he loved. Worse, the girls would lose it, without even the chance to make up their own minds about where they wanted to live. They would miss some of the best parts of Amish life. Miss the Sunday afternoon fellowship after church. Miss the frolics. The feeling of unity. Of belonging.

And what of Grace? Even if he left and got a divorce, would she leave her culture to follow him? He couldn't ask it of her.

Nee. He couldn't leave. And he would bring his wife home if, or more likely when, she asked.

Peter glanced toward the ceiling as he heard the scrape of furniture and occasional murmur of voices overhead as Grace put the girls to bed. Feeling decades older than his years, he pushed to his feet. He carefully refolded the letter and put it back into its envelope. The top drawer of the old desk screeched a protest as he pulled it out. Peter dropped the letter in and pushed the drawer closed. With a final look above to where the quiet murmurs were still audible, he trudged to the *daadi haus*.

Chapter Eleven

"Malinda and Fannie, before you go play with your dolls, carry your plates to the counter, please." A scrape of chairs against the linoleum accompanied the girls as they followed Grace's request before disappearing from the kitchen.

Peter frowned as he contemplated his own plate, mopped clean with a piece of fresh bread. He'd done his best to avoid Grace since receiving Lucetta's letter yesterday. He looked up to watch the back of the willowy young woman who worked at the counter. His frown deepened. What if his best wasn't *gut* enough? Should he send her away? The prospect made him wince. She was so *gut* for the girls. If things were different… He sighed. If things were different, she would have been so *gut* for him.

But they weren't. So something needed to change.

He drummed his fingers on the table. The girls had said Grace was looking for a beau. The reminder made the supper he'd just eaten congeal in his stomach. It took a series of shallow breaths to relieve the nauseous feeling.

Grace with a beau. In the few short years he'd been single, he had never poached other men's girls. If Grace belonged to someone else—Peter clenched his jaw at the notion—maybe he could forget his longing for her. He *had* to forget his longing for her.

At the sink, Grace was quietly humming a song he'd heard when he'd attended Singings years ago. Peter narrowed his eyes. Why didn't this attractive young woman have a beau in the first place? Were the men in the community blind?

He picked up his plate and glass, pushed back from the table and lunged to his feet. Grace looked over and smiled when he set his dinnerware on the counter. Her brows drew together when he crossed his arms over his chest and regarded her broodingly.

"Why haven't you married? I can't believe the single men of Miller's Creek, or wherever you're from in Iowa, haven't shown an interest."

Grace's cheeks grew rosy as she paid particular attention to setting the plug in the sink, starting the water and adding soap before she filled it with the glasses from dinner. For a moment, Peter didn't think she was going to respond. Heat spread up the back of his own neck as he reconsidered his outburst. He was taking a step back to spin on his heel and beat a hasty retreat when Grace's shoulders rose and fell on a small sigh.

"I thought I was well on my way to being married in Iowa." She cast him a sideways glance and worried her lower lip. "Are you sure you want to hear this?"

At his abrupt nod, she heaved another sigh. "My *mamm* has a best friend. The way they tell it, she and Edna have been close since they were still in their cradles. When they were young girls, they hatched a plan that one of their children would marry a child of the other. Edna married and had a series of daughters right away. But when my *mamm* married, she didn't have children for years. They were getting desperate."

Grace twisted her lips. "Finally, Edna had a son, Willis. To their relief, a short time later, I arrived. I was followed by several brothers, much to my *daed*'s relief, before I had a much younger sister. Willis ended up being the youngest one in his family."

It was quiet except for the clink of glasses as Grace washed and set them in the drainer and added plates to the water. "So, the only ones capable of fulfilling my *mamm* and Edna's dream were Willis and me. Before we knew of our mothers' arrangement, we didn't like each other all that much growing up."

"The catfish?"

Grace nodded and frowned, pausing in the midst of scrubbing a plate to gaze out the window. "Maybe I recognized even then that he was a bit—*ach*, more than a bit—spoiled, being the only son after a number of daughters. They all indulged him." She returned her attention to the dish, scrubbing it vigorously enough that Peter wondered if the faded flower pattern on it would survive.

"Just before we reached our teen years, we were advised of their plans for our lives. As Willis was a bit older than I, he was able to ignore them until I started my *rumspringa*."

While Peter quietly listened, he pulled a frayed dishtowel from where it hung on the stove handle and began to dry the plates in the drainer. When he realized what he was doing might be considered 'women's work', he mentally shrugged. He'd done the dishes when it'd been just him and the girls. It felt surprisingly peaceful working with Grace in the kitchen while the girls played contentedly in the other room. Another tantalizing glimpse of what he'd once imagined his married life would be like.

He froze. That was the last thing he should be thinking. There was no room for such imaginings in his life. He jerked into motion. Grace looked over when the plate clattered onto the counter.

She frowned. "You don't have to do that. I can take care of it."

Peter picked up another plate from the drainer. "That's all right. It feels… I don't like just standing here while you're working."

Her responding smile made him feel like the kitchen's temperature had risen by at least ten degrees. Peter carefully set down the dried plate on top of the other. The cozy scene was a temptation in itself. Should he retreat outside? Or at least into the other room? But he'd asked her a question and she was answering it. To leave at this point would be rude. Besides, to find her a beau, surely he needed to know why she didn't yet have one? And if he was a bit curious—well, more than a bit—there was that too.

Grace's gaze was questioning. When he ignored her to grab another plate and swipe the cloth over it, she shrugged. "At first, Willis avoided me at Singings and other frolics. Then, I imagine he started getting the same lectures at home that I was. He began asking to take me home." Grace rolled her eyes. "*Mamm* was up when we'd arrive. She always had some excuse, but she'd disappear right after we came into the house. I think she was checking so she could report back to Edna that Willis was doing as he was told."

She snorted softly. "Even though I was aware

of their plans, as a young girl, it was flattering to have a beau, even an unwilling one as things turned out, paying attention to me."

Grace swept a hand through the sink, seemingly focused on searching for residual dinnerware. Not finding any, she wrung out the dishcloth, strangling it until Peter doubted a single drop of water remained.

"I was trying to please my *mamm*. Trying to please everyone, I guess." She grimaced. "Although there were things about Willis that I wasn't even sure I liked, we were constantly pushed together with Edna and my *mamm*'s encouragement. Actually, more than encouragement. What is it when someone is doing all they can to get you to do something you're not sure you want to?"

"Manipulation." Intent on listening, the word popped out before Peter realized he'd spoken. "Coercion?" he offered, trying to keep the bitterness out of his voice.

Grace gave a wry smile as she walked backward to the kitchen table. "Well, it probably was, but my *mamm* dressed it up more prettily. Whatever the word, I finally convinced myself I was in love with Willis. That he was my special someone. That any day he was going to ask me to marry him. Though I don't know what I saw in him, other than the smiles on our mothers' faces whenever we were together."

"Would that have been enough?"

Grace's smile turned self-mocking. "I would have made it enough."

Peter frowned. Unlike his wife, Grace cared about making those she loved happy. Even at the cost of her own happiness.

Grace wiped off the table, cupping her hand along the edge of it to catch the crumbs that always accumulated at Fannie's location. "And though I had reservations whenever I was out of earshot of my *mamm*'s continued urging, I dreamed that we were going to live happily ever after."

Returning to the sink, she dropped the dishrag into it with a splash. "For sure and certain, Willis was planning his happily ever after. But it wasn't with me. And his *mamm* and mine weren't so happy when it was announced in church that he and Cora King were to be married a few weeks later."

Even her ears, visible in front of her pristine *kapp*, were now bright red. "I was so embarrassed I wanted to crawl under the church benches and escape unseen out the door. Out of the community. Even out of the county if possible. If everyone wasn't aware of what our mothers had been planning for years, folks knew from what *I'd* foolishly shared that I had planned on marrying Willis." She pulled the plug from the drain and stared at the sudsy water as it slowly disappeared.

Peter's grip tightened on the final plate until he was surprised the dish survived the pressure. He was intimately familiar with humiliation. He had been harnessed in tandem with it since shortly after his marriage to Lucetta. It was a weighty burden. Grace's embarrassment made him want to track down this Willis and remind him how to treat a young tenderhearted woman.

He added the plate to the stack and opened the cupboard door to shelve them. "They should be embarrassed for putting you into that situation. And him for leading you on when he had no plans to follow through."

Grace sent him a grateful smile, one encompassing her whole face—the still rosy cheeks, the expressive blue eyes…and the lovely upturned lips.

With a slow exhale, Peter focused his attention on shutting the wooden door with a quiet click. He turned away to hang the damp dishtowel over the oven door handle, his breathing shallow as he arranged it just so until he heard her move from beside him.

"I think my *mamm* was embarrassed. Maybe for herself." Peter turned in time to see Grace hunch a slender shoulder. "Maybe for me. At least she was flustered enough to let me accept the Miller's Creek teaching job when I begged her to let me leave the area. For which I was very grateful.

"But while I haven't forgotten my embarrassment, she's apparently forgotten hers. Willis's wife has died. As he's a widower now, they're at it again." Grace crossed her arms over her chest. "My *mamm* wrote me a letter. She wants me to come home to be courted by him. I couldn't bear to do so. But, as I said, I'm a bit of a—" she wrinkled her nose "—people pleaser. Sometimes, even though it might not be what is best for me, if it's what someone else wants me to do, I sometimes, *ach*, frequently, do it to please them."

She sighed gustily. "If I go home, I'm afraid I'll soon agree to *Mamm*'s plans. And who knows where things will end up this time. I'll be made a fool of again, or even worse, end up married to Willis. So, with school no longer in session, I needed an excuse to stay in Miller's Creek."

She grinned. "I'd just told Miriam my situation that day in church after Lydia fainted. And then there you came, and she suggested you give me a job."

"Is that what she was doing? Suggesting? I felt if I didn't accept she'd still have dropped you off here in the wee hours of the morning. Same thing when she and Aaron stopped by with the news of your flooded home."

At Grace's enticing giggle, Peter crossed his arms over his chest. If his hands were free, he was afraid they would reach for her. Pull her into his arms. Relish in her joy.

"She's become a *gut* friend. But she can be a bit…persuasive."

He wanted to hear her laugh again. The house had been devoid of the sound for years. A sound he'd recently, wonderfully, been hearing from his daughters. "Persuasive? I've seen cattle prods with less impact than her."

He succeeded. Peter was ready for it this time. Still, the sound seeped through him like warm maple syrup on hot pancakes.

After another brief giggle, Grace's gaze sobered. "Do you regret it? Giving me the job?"

"No." Peter shook his head. *But I should. For sure and certain, I will before all is said and done.* "The girls are happy. And I…it gives me more time with them, and to work the farm when I don't have to travel to Lydia's twice a day."

"Well, you just learned that you're doing me a big favor by giving me a job over the summer so I don't have to go home."

Peter jerked a nod in acknowledgment. After hearing Grace's story, he couldn't let her go back to that situation. But, so engrossed in her story, he'd forgotten his initial purpose for this conversation. He rubbed a hand over the back of his neck. "I can understand why you left Iowa. You've been here for a few years though, *ja*? You're...well." He clumsily gestured toward her. "What about the men here?"

Her brow furrowed. "What about them?"

"Why aren't you walking out with one of them? The girls mentioned they heard you say you were looking for a beau."

Grace clapped her hands to her cheeks. "I did not! When did they say this?"

"That day coming home from church."

Grace closed her eyes, apparently trying to remember that morning. After a moment, they popped open. "Oh. That was another suggestion of Miriam's. She was trying to think of any reason that my mother would accept to allow me to stay."

Peter frowned. "Then you aren't looking for a beau?"

"It's not like I go shopping for one like I was browsing along the aisles at the Piggly Wiggly."

"But you would go out if one asked?"

Grace eyed him oddly before pursing her lips. "Maybe I'm not yet ready." She made a show of looking out the window toward the lane. "But even if I was, I don't see anyone lining up to do so."

Peter grunted. He, too, glanced out the window

toward the empty lane before he retreated to the common room. Single men might not be lining up now. But they would by the time he was finished. He hoped it would be enough to remind him that, though she was here, she wasn't, and could never be, his.

Chapter Twelve

Peter gripped the two pieces of curved metal in one hand as he slid his other, damp with sweat, down the side of his pants. He glanced longingly over his shoulder to where Hazel, already slouch-hipped for her wait, was tied to the hitching post.

This was a foolish thing to do. Grace had even said yesterday that she might not be ready.

But he was. Ready to end the disturbance her presence stirred in him. Surely even if Grace stayed physically near, if she was no longer emotionally available because she had a beau, she wouldn't unsettle him so. Would she?

He transferred the heavy metal pieces to swipe his hands again. He just wasn't ready to walk into Reihl and Sons' Smithy and find her one. But, as he could hear the rhythmic clang of a hammer inside, they would've heard Hazel's hooves clatter on the gravel when he'd come up the lane. In fact, either Thomas or his son Noah would've glanced out the window at his arrival and were probably wondering what he was doing dawdling in their yard.

With a shoulder-lifting sigh, Peter trudged toward the smithy door. He'd spent the night staring at the ceiling of the little bedroom in the *daadi haus* as he contemplated all the single men he knew in both their community and the surrounding areas. One by one, he'd discarded the candidates. They weren't good enough for Grace for one reason or another. The shadowed ceiling had seemed to mock him when he'd discovered he'd weeded them all out and had to begin again. Upon second review, Noah Reihl had topped the list.

Noah had returned the previous spring to help expand his *daed*'s blacksmith business. Whereas the business had previously been too small to support more than just Thomas, Noah had ideas to expand it beyond local farming needs. The Reihls now made and shipped small metalwork pieces to where Thomas's older son, who lived in a larger, more touristy community, sold them to the *Englisch*. To Peter's mind, Noah had shown himself to be loyal, resourceful and steadily employed.

There'd been nothing on the Amish grapevine to indicate Noah participated in more than the normal amount of supposedly secret buggy races than other unmarried men did. No knowing jokes among *youngies* in their *rumspringa*, nor frowning comments among the older set to imply he was involved in the types of parties, Amish or beyond, that Lucetta had favored.

What if the man already had a sweetheart? Peter paused as he reached for the door handle. Well, she couldn't be better than Grace. A bead of sweat trickled down his back. And he couldn't feel any more foolish than he already did. Peter sucked in a breath. He hoped.

"*Guder nummidaag*, Peter." Thomas greeted him as he stepped through the door. "Noah and I were wondering if you were going to come in or whether you'd just stopped by to check out the yard."

"Good afternoon to you too, Thomas. Well, if I was checking it out, it's because it's a *gut* example of what a well-run farm should look like." Peter set the two pieces of the broken tooth on the rough wooden bench.

The older blacksmith set his hammer down on the end of the anvil and strode over to inspect the new arrivals on the bench. "You're a hard worker. You'll get there. Some things just take a little time."

Though Peter didn't want to think he needed to hear the words, they were a balm to his tattered confidence. "A little time and, at the moment, more than a little help."

Thomas frowned as he examined the two pieces. "This looks like a clean break. Were you able to finish harrowing? Or do you need this soon in order to get to planting?"

Peter tugged at the neck of his shirt as he recalled the effort he'd had to apply to break the tooth in order to have an excuse to visit the blacksmith. *I'm working on planting. Working on planting the thoughts of courtship into someone's head.* The prospect twisted like hot metal in his stomach. "I finished enough to plant. Pretty well done there too, though I'll have to see if any drowned out in the low spots with the storm the other day."

He glanced over to where Noah was working on the far side of the small shop. The young man gave him a nod, which Peter returned. *How am I to get Noah alone so I can convince him to court Grace?* He turned back to Thomas. "How are Cilla and Emma doing?"

The man's bearded face split into a smile at the mention of the granddaughter he hadn't known existed until last year and the spinster next door he'd married since then. "Couldn't be finer."

Searching for another topic, Peter glanced about the shop and spied a tray of, amongst other crafted items, belt buckles, their design simple but striking. Obviously, something for the *Englisch*, as Amish didn't wear belts. He stepped closer to nudge one with his finger. "This business with the *Englisch* going well?"

"*Ja*. Can't complain. Seems like some don't know what they need until you bring it to their attention."

Peter rubbed a hand over his mouth. Without asking Noah to follow him into the yard, it would be impossible to avoid an audience. Besides, Thomas was no fool. If he used some awkward excuse to do so, Noah might tell his father anyway as the man would surely be curious.

Was it worth this embarrassment to try to find Grace a beau? Peter was sweating so much even his toes were perspiring in his work boots. He shifted his weight to pivot for the door. The memory of how difficult it had been to leave her and walk out of the house the night of the storm stopped him. *Ja*. It was worth it.

He cleared his throat. "Well, something every man needs is a *gut* wife."

Thomas and Noah eyed him warily, as if unsure of how to respond. Everyone in the community knew of his wife troubles. Everyone knew he didn't speak of them.

Thomas finally nodded. "Having had two, first Priscilla and now Emma, I can agree with you there."

His chest tight, Peter turned to the younger

man. "How about you, Noah? You in need of a *gut* wife?"

Noah set down his hammer and grinned. "Why? You know of one available?"

Peter had to swallow hard to get past the lump in his throat at pushing Grace in the direction of another man. "I might."

Grace lifted the big pot of chicken and dumplings from the floor of the buggy. Would it and what else she brought be enough? She hadn't had much time to prepare, as Peter had come back from the blacksmith shop only a day ago to report that the work frolic was scheduled for today. Glancing over her shoulder, she eyed the buggies lined up along the lane of her schoolteacher lodging and calculated the number of men who might be working to repair the floor. Surely the small space available inside would limit their number?

While she was brushing the girls' hair and pinning it up in their *kapps*, Peter had carried the food to her buggy before hitching up both horses and setting off himself. He had said she'd fixed too much, but he was in one of his winter moods, so she ignored his comment.

With a sigh, she lugged the heavy pot across the yard, Malinda and Fannie trailing in her wake carrying baskets, one of rolls and the other, oatmeal cookies and whoopie pies. They headed for a makeshift table of plywood straddling two saw-horses that she'd asked Peter to arrange prior to her arrival. Grace set the pot down with a thud on top of the tablecloth she'd earlier draped over the plywood. With a smile for the girls, she added their items.

Another rig pulled into the yard as she returned to the buggy for the next load. Grace smiled when Miriam descended from its interior. They met at the makeshift table as both deposited their contributions. Aaron handed Miriam their toddler before returning for more items.

The girls were delighted to see the little one. "Can we take him into the yard?"

"*Ja*, Malinda. He'd enjoy that." Miriam set her son down, maintaining her hold until his chubby legs were steady. "Just stay away from where the men are working." Malinda nodded solemnly. She and Fannie each took one of the little boy's hands and guided him into the yard.

Grace touched Miriam on the forearm. "*Denki*, for your help. As it's, in a sense, my house, I figured that made me the hostess of this frolic. I'm afraid I've forgotten something, and with all the men in the house and no floor besides, I doubt I can get anything from the kitchen."

"It will be fine. Esther Zook is coming with things, as well as my sister-in-law, Gail. We'll have plenty." Miriam looked over to where some men were cutting lumber as others carried the pieces into the house. "Too bad the whole floor had to be replaced. But they should get it done today, except for the new water heater. Aaron says it isn't here yet." She turned back to Grace with a smile. "I'm sure you'll be glad to move back in."

Grace turned to look as well, automatically finding where Peter was measuring a length of board. Watching him, she burst into tears.

"What…?"

Pressing trembling lips together, Grace glanced back to Miriam, who stared at her with wide eyes.

"Oh help." Miriam slowly shook her head. "I never expected this to happen. You're in love with him."

Grace dipped her chin in a nod as hot tears trickled down her cheeks. She jerked a corner of her apron up to dab at them as Aaron approached with a large pot.

"That should be it." The table groaned as he set it down. He looked at Grace before turning to his wife with a frown. "What's the matter with her?"

Grace ducked her head and turned her back to him.

"Ah, she's just looking forward to getting back into her house and worried, the way you men eat, that there won't be enough to feed you all today."

"It looks like there's enough to me. But just to be certain, I'll make sure I'm first in line."

"You're not helping, Aaron." Miriam's voice was as dry as the piles of sawdust that were growing under the working men.

"*Ach*, you'd think I'd learn not to tease weepy women. Um, Grace?"

Grace hunched her shoulders but didn't turn around.

"I'll get out here with the water heater the day it arrives so you can get moved back in." Quick footsteps revealed Aaron's hasty retreat.

Miriam slipped her arm around Grace's shoulders and walked her to the far side of the house. "This is my fault. I threw you two together. I never imagined." She shook her head again. "Though reserved, Peter is an appealing man. I should have realized."

"It's not your fault." Grace blotted at a fresh batch of tears. "I never imagined either. I didn't even like him at first. But I got to know him and I…" She sniffed. "I know it's hopeless."

Miriam squeezed her shoulder. "Do you want to get away? Do you want me to tell him that you need to stop watching the girls? I imagine Lydia can take them again. Or they can come to my house?"

"I accepted this job. I love caring for the girls. And if I wasn't, well, without the job, what would be my reason for not returning to Iowa for the summer? Or forever," Grace added glumly. She dropped the corner of her apron and tried to smooth out its wrinkles. "During the day, it's not so bad. He's out working except for mealtime, when the girls are there. But I guess it would be a good idea to avoid him as much as possible, feeling like I do."

"You can stay at our house until yours is ready. It's what I should have suggested first. You get your things tonight and bring them over."

Grace swallowed. There it was again. Another person's recommendation that she could easily fall in with. One that would meet Miriam's approval and would even answer part of her problem. Grace opened her mouth to accept before shutting it with a click of her teeth. But was it what she wanted? Or needed? Wasn't she capable of tending to her own issues?

With a quivering smile, she straightened her back and slipped out from underneath Miriam's supportive arm. "*Denki*. That is tempting. And I just might show up at your door. But let me think it over for a bit."

"Whatever you need. I just want to help." Miriam smiled wryly. "Aaron thinks sometimes that I overhelp. He would've been right on this one. Don't tell him."

Grace pressed her hands to her cheeks. "The

last thing I want to have happen is anyone finding out about my foolishness."

Miriam's expression sobered. "They won't from me. I'm so sorry, Grace, for getting you into this situation."

Peter marked the measurement with a flat pencil. He nodded to Gideon Schrock on the other end of the lumber, who let go of the tape measure. With a quiet rattle, the metal tape slithered back across the board's surface as it recoiled.

He was relieved Gideon was here today. It saved him from trying to track the man down. It had been bad enough talking about Grace to Noah while the man's father was listening. He couldn't imagine doing the same where Gideon worked at Schrock Brothers' Furniture with an audience of Gideon's *bruder* Malachi and several others.

Noah had seemed interested, but Grace deserved options. Gideon was his reluctant second choice as a beau for her. Peter eyed the blond-haired, blue-eyed man as he carried cut lumber into the house. It wasn't that Gideon didn't have qualities. He had a *gut* job. Was a hard worker. Easygoing and well liked, he was amusing and *gut* company. But that was the problem. He was such *gut* amusing company that the community's single women fluttered about him. Which Gideon didn't seem to mind at all. In fact, he encouraged it. The man didn't seem to take much seriously. Including the business of settling down.

Peter didn't want a flirt for Grace. Especially one who might dally with her while he dallied with someone else. She'd already had that. Already been hurt by that. Which was why Gideon wasn't at the top of Peter's list. But while the man might be a flirt, Peter had never heard that he'd broken the heart of anyone's sisters or daughters.

He worked with Gideon throughout the morning and, when dinner was called, collected a plate of food—carefully avoiding Grace—and sauntered with the blond man to take a seat under a nearby tree.

Stabbing a dumpling with his fork, Peter eyed his companion. "I didn't figure to see you here, fixing up the house for the school board. My older girl is going into school this fall. But you don't even have any *kinner*." His brow's lowered. "Do you?"

Gideon looked startled before breaking into a grin. "*Nee*. I'm just serving as a stand-in. Lillian is school-aged, but Samuel couldn't make it because he was delivering a horse today. Malachi let me off work to represent the Schrocks, as between those two, they'll probably have several *kinner* go through school in the years to come."

Peter focused on his plate and the food he had

no appetite for. "What about you? You plan on getting married and having a family soon?"

Gideon laughed. "You're sounding like my sister and sisters-in-law. They keep trying to get me married off."

"There…" Peter bit his tongue. Affected by the man's good nature, he'd almost quipped that there were worst things than getting married. But there wasn't. Not based on his history. Not when he'd gotten married to the wrong woman. But Grace wasn't a wrong woman. She'd just never be *his* woman.

He cleared his throat. "There are some pretty *gut* options out there." Though he ached in doing so, he let his gaze land on where Grace smiled as she dished up another worker's plate. Gideon followed his gaze. He dipped his chin in acknowledgment.

"Easy on the eye. *Gut* with children. Hardworking." Peter's stomach twisted as he voiced Grace's attributes. *Patient, encouraging, smart, spirited, sincere, charming.*

Gideon's lips twitched. "You selling? I've heard auctioneers with less patter."

Peter's face flamed. "She's not mine to sell. Grace has been working at my house for the last while. Just seems like she would make someone a *gut* wife. I'm surprised she isn't walking out with someone."

His flush deepened as Gideon turned to scrutinize him from the top of his flat-brimmed straw hat to the soles of his scuffed work boots. Peter scowled. "What?"

"Matchmaking? You just seem a little tall and skinny for that short, chubby *Englisch* character that flies around shooting little arrows into hearts."

Peter pushed to his feet before bending to pick up his plate. "I'm no cupid."

As he stalked away, Gideon's laugh and parting words followed him. "Could have fooled me."

Chapter Thirteen

When they were back at work, every time Peter would look up, Gideon would be watching him. And smiling. It was difficult to concentrate on his work when blood continually deserted his brain to brighten the back of his neck to a perennial red. He'd had to measure one length three times before he marked it and made a cut, much to the blond man's amusement.

His discomfiture deepened when Josiah Lapp emerged from the little house. After relaying the needed cut size of chipboard to finish up inside, the young man drawled, "So, I hear you're recruiting beaus for the schoolteacher. Where do I sign up?"

Peter jerked at the question, almost sawing off his finger. While debating his list of potential beaus, Josiah, of a good family and around Grace's age, had crossed his mind. But he'd quickly been deleted from consideration. If Gideon seemed a fair distance from settling down, Josiah was miles from doing so. Malinda would probably be in her *rumspringa* before Josiah was ready to be serious about a girl.

Peter lifted his head to frown at Gideon. Though he laughed, Gideon shook his head.

"I didn't tell him. But he wasn't standing too far off from where we were eating dinner, and those big ears of his have to be *gut* for something." Gideon's voice was obviously pitched for the younger man's hearing, even before he turned to face the newcomer with a grin. "If there's an invitation to walk out with the schoolteacher, it's for grown-ups, Josiah. Not for those who have the mentality to still be in her classroom. Mature men only."

Josiah propped his hands on lean hips. "And he's asking you? We've got heifers in our dairy herd that are more mentally mature than you are."

"Maybe you should date them then. But I've heard that their conversation is more intelligent than yours," Gideon countered.

Though he cringed at the discussion's topic, Peter had to duck his head and cough to cover his stifled snort.

"Besides," Gideon continued, "just like on the ball field, you're too slow, Josiah. You'll have to wait your turn on this, *if* you get to have one." Realizing he was momentarily outmatched, Josiah shook his head good-naturedly as he hefted the chipboard and returned to the house.

Peter's eyes widened. Had Gideon already asked Grace to walk out? His mouth went dry at the possibility. It was one thing to conceive of the plan of Grace belonging to someone else. It was something else to have it actually happen. Just because it was the right thing to do didn't make it more palatable.

He shot a glance at Gideon, frowning when the man met it with a wink. What did *that* mean? Though his chest was tight with the desire to know if the two had already made an arrangement to get together, fear of the answer was greater. Peter kept his thoughts to himself. They were not good company.

To Grace's relief, by the time the women had finished with their meals, the men had the subflooring down, making a surface the woman could use in the kitchen. With water heated on the stove, they did dishes there while the men took an afternoon break.

When Grace exited the kitchen, the men assigned to install the underlayment and linoleum tiles to finish the day's work filed past her. They all gave her a nod and a smile. Actions she reciprocated until the last one winked at her. Blinking in surprise, Grace looked over her shoulder to watch as the young man disappeared through the doorway.

What was that about? Smiles I can understand. They're working on my house. But a wink?

Shrugging her shoulder, Grace headed to the sawhorse table to collect her supplies. As she crossed the yard, she checked on where the girls were contentedly playing under a tree. The glance she sent to where Peter was collecting his tools was more covert and much longer.

Grace sighed. Miriam surely thought she was a ninny, bursting into tears the way she had. Then to have her friend realize she was in love with Peter... Grace pressed her palms to her cheeks, ones that flamed again with embarrassment. She pushed her hands up to rub her forehead. But Miriam was right. She shouldn't stay at Peter's home overnight any longer. Should she just leave them altogether? The back of her eyes prickled at the possibility. Grace squeezed them shut and sniffed.

She should. But could she? There was something about staying with the Lehmans, a belonging Grace hadn't felt in a long time. She was needed. She was wanted. Not for just her physical presence, but for herself. Grace. She wasn't ready to leave the girls. She wasn't ready to leave their father. But loving him and knowing there was no hope for any good outcome, was it worth the pain of staying?

Grace opened her eyes to see the jumble of

supplies she'd brought on the makeshift table. Shoulders slumped, she gathered the items and carried them in a series of trips to the buggy. After situating the last load, she leaned against the back wheel and swiped her wrist over her forehead to blot away perspiration from the warm day. Her gaze landed on the dented mailbox at the end of the lane.

She groaned. "I forgot to let the mailman know I wasn't staying here." Pushing up from the wheel, she headed toward the lane. Very little mail should have arrived during her time away. She had no bills. Only correspondence with some folks she'd met in the few years she'd been teaching here and with friends and cousins she kept in touch with in Iowa.

Her steps slowed on the gravel.

And there might be a response to the letter. The one, after having delayed as long as possible, she'd finally sent off to her mother. The one stating she wouldn't be home for the summer. Well, stating was perhaps an exaggeration. It was more of a strong hint. She'd explained that a church member had needed help caring for his children. As she'd been free for the summer and, as *Gott* desires us to help our neighbor, she'd agreed to assist him. If she'd made it sound like she'd agreed to take the job before receiving her *mamm*'s initial letter, well, that was unfortunate and couldn't be corrected now. Either way, she couldn't come home and participate in her *mamm*'s scheme.

Grace stared at the rounded metal door of the mailbox. Finally, she lifted a hand to the little hook. The door opened with a *creak* to reveal a small collection of envelopes inside. With the enthusiasm and hesitancy she would have used to remove a mouse from a trap, Grace reached in to take them. One by one, she flipped through the letters, breathing a little more easily with each one. Until she came to the last.

Grace didn't need to check the return address to know where it came from. Her own address was an unhappy slash across the front. She drew in a deep breath. That didn't necessarily mean her *mamm* was disturbed with her news, did it? She tucked the other letters under her arm and, worrying her lower lip, opened the one from her mother.

It did. Grace could almost hear her mother lecturing her as she read the lines.

If you want a job watching someone else's children, you could easily find one in our own district. And, very shortly, you could even be taking care of your own children. If you would just come home. I'm sure the widower can find someone else to watch his daughters.

Grace grimaced. She'd left her situation open to a few assumptions. Peter's wedded state for one.

But her sense of guilt was balanced by her *mamm*'s next line: *Willis has been asking about you.*

Ha. That was an exaggeration if she'd ever heard one. Willis probably didn't even remember her. Or wouldn't, if their mothers didn't keep nagging in his ear.

Grace tilted her head back until her face was warmed by the afternoon sun. If she kept her job with Peter, she would face heartache at seeing him every day and knowing what could never be. If she left her job, she'd have no excuse to stay in Miller's Creek. And therefore, no reason not to return to Iowa, where she would either succumb to her mother's plans and face more embarrassment when Willis again rejected her, or worse, actually marry him. Or more unlikely, she'd somehow gain the courage to refuse and then forever endure her mother's obvious disappointment and disapproval.

Grace tapped the letter against her palm. She loved her *mamm*. But she was weary of allowing herself to be driven, led, tugged and shoved into someone else's plans. She knew herself though. Whether it was lack of courage, or just the desire to please, if she went home, she would eventually fall in with them.

Of the two options, there was no question. Grace closed the metal door, retrieved the rest of the letters from under her arm and stuck her *mamm*'s letter in the back of them before heading up the lane.

She didn't want to leave Peter yet anyway.

"Are you sure you'll be all right?"

"*Ja.* My *mamm* left us alone a lot." Malinda didn't look up from where she was tucking her doll, along with Fannie's, into an old wooden cradle. "And we were littler then."

Grace winced at the girl's response. Like many Amish children, with the exception of their reluctance with the hens, Malinda and Fannie were capable of many responsibilities that *Englischers* might think exceeded their ages. But still, she hurt for them for their history with their mother.

"All right. I shouldn't be long."

Only long enough to tell Peter that, even though the water heater still wasn't installed, she was moving back into her rented house. Tonight.

She didn't appreciate what she'd heard yesterday afternoon. The news Miriam had shared, her eyes wide as she'd exited the little house with a last load of dishes. The conversations of those inside had been about Grace. Even now, recalling the smiles and the wink she'd received at the work frolic, her stomach twisted.

Peter was soliciting beaus for her. He had been asking the community's single men if they'd consider walking out with her. Well, a few of them at least. But one was too many. Too much a reminder of her *mamm* arranging a beau for her.

Peter hadn't even had the nerve to come in last night and admit his folly. When she'd heard his buggy come up the lane, she'd braced herself to face him. But Peter had carefully timed his visit to the house, ducking in to say goodnight to the girls before disappearing into the *daadi haus* while she'd been busy in the kitchen. He'd even missed supper.

If she wasn't so embarrassed by his actions, she'd be hurt by his avoidance.

She'd spent a sleepless night. Why did everyone think they could do a better job of planning her life? Though Grace was up early, she hadn't caught Peter this morning. He'd already grabbed a slice of bread and escaped to the barn. Silently fuming, interspersed with anxious glances out the window to ensure he didn't retreat farther to the field, Grace waited until the girls had gotten up and been fed. They were finally settled. Now it was time to talk with their father.

Squaring her shoulders, she marched out the door and across the farmyard. She had last seen him releasing the Standardbred horses and the cow out into the pasture before returning to the barn.

Just because she had told him she had a habit of falling in with other's suggestions, did he think she'd be pleased with what he was doing? He hadn't even bothered to advise her of his plan before plunging into it. At least her *mamm* had been upfront about what she'd been doing.

She slowed to a halt as she approached the big double doors. Had Peter discovered how she felt about him? She cupped her hands over her mouth. Had she let something slip? Had he intercepted one of her covert looks? That was mortifying enough. What if he was trying to get her to leave before she embarrassed them both with her obvious longing?

She wanted to sink through the scant gravel that covered the farmyard. Would she never learn to keep her thoughts to herself regarding men? At least Peter wouldn't humiliate her by marrying someone else. Ha. He already had.

Did his public search humiliate her enough to quit her job and go back to Iowa? *Nee*. Loving Peter was foolish, but at least she liked him as well, which was more than she could say for Willis. Grace clenched her fists. Regardless of how she felt, she needed to tell Peter she was going home this evening. That he was on his own with the girls at night. And if the other issue came up, well, they needed to talk about that too. But first, she had to find him.

* * *

Peter glanced out the big hayloft door to see Grace coming across the yard. There was no doubt she was looking for him. She wasn't heading for the coop to feed the chickens and gather the eggs. She'd already done that. He knew, because as soon as she'd stepped into the coop with her basket, he'd hustled the full milk can to the house so he wouldn't have to do it later when she might catch him from the kitchen.

He didn't want to call himself a coward, but for sure and certain, he was wearing the shoes and hat of one. From the set expression on Grace's face, it seemed like a *gut* idea to keep them on a little longer. He'd lived for years avoiding Lucetta whenever possible, weary of her continued belittling and complaining. His belly gained another knot until it contained as many as the twine that corralled the loft's hay. He was avoiding Grace not because of what had been done to him, but because of the hurt and embarrassment he'd caused her. How did one apologize for something like that?

Peter sighed as he sped down the wooden ladder from the loft fast enough to draw splinters. He hadn't thought about others overhearing his conversation with Gideon yesterday. Unfortunately, Josiah Lapp wasn't known for his discretion. Gideon had taken the afternoon's ribbing in good stride. Maybe too good. Him, not so much. What had he put in motion? One didn't need to be *schtupid* to realize Grace had found out what he had done. Which is why he'd avoided her last night and this morning. And intended to do so now.

Peter froze at the bottom of the ladder. What if his actions drove her away? What if she was coming out to tell him she was leaving? It was entirely possible. His hands curled about the worn wood. If that's what she was coming to tell him, he didn't want to hear that either.

He turned from the loft ladder to stare across the barn. Where could he go where she wouldn't follow? His gaze landed on the small door to the grain silo. The silo with the large clump of grain that still needed to be cleaned out. Corn that was stuck and therefore useless. Like Lucetta had constantly reminded him he was. Failures she'd pointed out over the years thundered through his thoughts. And now he'd wronged Grace. At least he could do something about the grain situation. Now was as good a time as any. In fact, as access to the silo's interior was limited, now was even better.

With a wary glance at the barn's door, willing it to stay closed, Peter strode to his tool room and retrieved the long-handled, flat metal-scraping tool he used to clean the edges of the stalls. He jerked a short wooden ladder from where it hung along the wall and carried both out the side door of the barn, the ladder banging against his legs in his haste.

The front of the barn was blocked from view by the round silo. If he couldn't see Grace, she couldn't see him. Sheepish at his evasion, Peter set the scraper down as he eyed the old metal ladder that began farther up the concrete wall's exterior. He steadied the wooden ladder beneath it, snatched the scraper and started up the rungs. As he transitioned from the wooden to the metal ladder, he heard Grace call his name. Peter hesitated. He stepped back to the wooden rung. Biting the inside of his cheek, he grimly climbed up.

When Peter didn't answer her tentative call, Grace pushed one side of the barn door open. She heard the stomp of the Belgians' big hooves against a stall floor, a quiet grunt from one of the hogs, and the cooing of some pigeons in the loft, but nothing to indicate Peter's location.

"Peter?"

Her call echoed in the cavernous space. Grace entered the barn, counting the draft horses in their stalls as she passed. Along with Bella and her foal, they were all accounted for, so Peter hadn't gone into the field. She crossed to the big mare, who greeted her arrival by hanging her huge head over the stall wall for a pat. Grace provided one, in addition to a scratch or two on Tanner's baby-fluffed rump, as she scanned the visible recesses of the barn.

"Where is he, Bella? Do you know?"

At the sound of a muted rattle, the mare turned her head toward the rounded gray concrete that made up part of the barn's far wall. Grace followed the mare's gaze. Furrowing her brow as she listened intently, she headed in that direction. The rattle and clanging increased in volume as she reached a small metal door about waist high set in the concrete. Below the door, a large cart was tucked along the wall. A handful of yellow corn kernels were splayed over its bottom. More kernels were scattered on the ground alongside its wheels. Beneath the cart was another opening, blocked by the emergence of a rusty auger.

Grace rubbed a hand over her forehead as she considered the metal door. If the silo beyond it had grain above that level, should she slide it open, gravity would send the corn pouring out and maybe even prevent her from getting the door closed again. She'd no longer have to worry that Peter would let her go, as there would certainly be no doubt if she filled his barn with corn and buried the nearby pigs.

Another *clang*, this time accompanied by a soft *thunk*. Grace tipped her ear next to the small door. It was definitely coming from inside. She lifted a hand and tentatively rapped on the metal. It rattled slightly under her knock. Surely if grain were pressed against its back, it wouldn't do so? At her tap, the rattle and clanging inside the silo abruptly stopped. Bracing herself to shove it back if corn poured through, Grace wrapped her hands around the door's rusted metal handle and tugged.

With a reluctant *screech*, the metal slid a fraction, releasing the earthy smell of field corn and dust. Standing to the side, Grace jerked it open wider, turning her head as a cloud of dust rolled out. When nothing else joined it, she moved the cart out of the way before returning to the small door to squat to its height and peer inside.

A carpet of golden yellow corn covered the bin a few inches lower than the level of the door. Grace's gaze swept the gray walls before landing on the large mass of corn that clung to the silo's far wall. No sign of what had generated the noise could be seen from her angle. *Where was he?* Grace inhaled sharply, the dust tickling her nose and making her sneeze, before, with compressed lips, she stuck her head and shoulders into the opening.

Now she could see a fragile metal ladder emerging from the mass. Hanging onto it with one hand while the other grasped a long wooden handle was Peter...who didn't look happy to see her.

Even from his location several yards away and an equal distance above her, Grace saw his jaw tighten. Turning his shoulder to her, he jerked the wooden handle up enough to reveal its flat metal end before stabbing it back into the golden-yellow mass. Corn fell from it in trickles and occasional chunks. Grace squinted against the dust the small avalanches raised. Peter's shoulders hunched as he coughed. The metal ladder creaked as he shifted in his position.

He was going to ignore her. Grace frowned as her gaze traveled up the rungs until, almost at the domed roof, she saw the ladder originated from a small opening in the wall. She pursed her lips. With her blocking one exit and the other very much out of the way, it would be difficult for him to escape.

Peter seemed to recognize that as well. The ladder rattled and banged with his jabs into the corn, sometimes bouncing away from the concrete wall with his effort. Grace eyed it—and Peter's precarious perch—warily as more corn cascaded down. She held her breath when the ladder shook as another large golden chunk broke off and plummeted.

"Don't come in here," he warned without turning around.

"What are you doing?" Her call reverberated up the silo.

"What does it look like? I'm trying to get the corn down. I put it up too wet last fall and it consolidated." Peter's back remained toward her. He kept chipping away, his back shaking with an occasional cough.

Grace scanned the bin's interior. Was there a less dangerous option? Maybe Peter could get the old auger to work? Would that pull the corn down? "Is this the best way to do so?"

That stopped him. Peter's broad shoulders rose and fell in an exaggerated sigh. "I thought I was finished with a woman continually criticizing me when my wife left." He finally turned to glare down at her. "You have a better idea?"

The comparison to Lucetta stung. As did the insinuation that she had a habit of criticizing. "I don't know. The ones you come up with, like asking the district's single men to walk out with me—" the bite in Grace's voice bounced off the walls "—seem pretty questionable."

His shoulders visibly tensing under his dusty white shirt, Peter attacked the corn with renewed vigor. It came off in slabs. He stepped down a rung on the ladder to reach the newly exposed edge.

Grace squeezed her eyes shut, blocking out the dust and the sight of the stubborn man. Just like you could lead a horse to water but you couldn't make him drink, it seemed you could corner a man, but you couldn't make him talk. Why didn't that surprise her with this one?

She opened her eyes to squint at his form, still several feet above her in the escalating dust. Grace sighed. "I just came to tell you I've decided to go back home."

Peter went completely still. Except for the acoustics in the silo, she wouldn't have heard his quiet question, as it was directed to the fragile ladder in front of him. "To Iowa?"

"Nee." Grace's stomach clenched at the thought. "My rented house is ready enough. I'm going there tonight."

Grace didn't think he was going to answer. Again, she had the silo to thank for amplifying his low-voiced response. "You coming back to-morrow?"

It was silent except for the sound of corn slithering down to pool onto the existing carpet of gold.

"I'd like to."

Peter gave a brief nod before reaching out to jab again into the corn. Grace stared at his back. Was he not even going to turn around? Was he glad or irritated that she was coming back? She scowled. At least she still seemed to have a job, but it looked like that was all the acknowledgment she was going to get. If it wasn't so dusty, she was tempted to stick her tongue out at him. Well, she said what she came to say.

Shifting backward, she started to duck out of the small opening when a rumble reverberated through the silo. Grace froze as a large section of corn peeled off, pulling part of the ladder, with Peter on it, from the wall.

Chapter Fourteen

Grace screamed as the avalanching corn roared down. Kernels pelted her face. She jerked her head back, her hairpins digging into her scalp when it banged against the wall. Wincing, Grace pressed a hand to her crushed *kapp* and the other over her mouth and nose as she peered through the thick dust.

Where was Peter?

Heartbeat pounding in her ears, she scoured the floor of the silo for any break in the relentless golden yellow. Was he buried? How deep? If she found him, could she reach him before he suffocated?

The rain of corn subsided until only a muted slithering sound indicated a few small waterfalls of movement remained. Grace's eyes were filled with grit. She forced them open, her breathing shallow behind her fingers as she searched for Peter. Corn trickled past her hips and scattered onto the barn floor behind her as she scrabbled for a better foothold to climb through the small opening.

The avalanche had spread corn over the floor of the bin, with a higher pile in the center. Thankfully the small door hadn't been buried, but a new layer of corn was wedged under Grace's elbows.

Dust still hovered heavily as she wiggled her way into the bin.

"Peter?" Her call echoed up the chamber. "Peter!" On hands and knees, she scrambled over the corn. It was a moment before she looked up to see that most of the mass had already fallen and no longer loomed dangerously overhead. Only a danger to the one who'd fallen with it.

Her hand sank through the shifting floor to touch something that wasn't grain. With a choking gasp, Grace hastily swept away the corn to unearth the brim of Peter's hat. She pulled it out, but though she frantically continued to dig, she didn't find anything else. The dust was slowly settling. Grace sat back on her heels to scan the area.

On the far side of the center pile, something was protruding from the corn. Grace scurried over to discover a broken section of the rusty ladder. Beside it, framed by golden yellow, was Peter's face. Grace briefly burst into tears even as she lifted a hand to carefully brush a few kernels from his closed eyes. Other than the smear of blood oozing from a cut on his forehead, his face was as pale as her *kapp*.

"Oh, Peter." Grace scooted to the side to ensure she wasn't kneeling where his chest might be hidden beneath the corn. With cupped hands, she began to dig him out. She had to drag the corn away the length of her arms to prevent it from trickling back on top of him. Grace closed her eyes briefly in relief to discover only a few inches of grain covered his shirt. Clearing it away, she rested a cautious hand on his chest between his suspenders. More tears leaked when it rose and fell with his shallow breathing.

She was so focused on the movement that at first she didn't register the sound coming from inside the barn.

"Miss Kauffman? Are you here? Miss Kauffman? I've brought Sunny over."

Grace whipped her head toward the little door. "In here, James!" She stifled a sob. *Thank You, Gott!* Holding her breath, she listened as the sound of footsteps hesitantly approached the silo. The metal door rattled as it was pushed farther open. A moment later James Yoder poked his head through. At the sight of his frowning face, Grace forgave every prank the young man had ever pulled in her classroom.

"I heard you scream." His eyes rounded as he

took in the situation. "What can I do to help? I'm too big to fit through this opening."

"When the corn came down, the ladder, with Peter on it, fell too. Race Sunny to the phone shack and call Gabe, the EMT. Peter is breathing, but I don't know where all he is hurt. We have to get him help."

James nodded. He cast a grim look around the silo's interior. Grace didn't need him to tell her that it would be difficult for help to get to Peter. And even more difficult to safely get him out.

"Hurry!" She called as he disappeared from the opening.

It seemed an eternity until Grace heard the faint sound of a siren outside. She had passed the time by carefully uncovering Peter until his arms and legs were exposed. She'd removed her apron and used it to stop the bleeding on his forehead and the hem of her dress to wipe the corn dust from his eyes, nose and mouth.

Peter hadn't opened his eyes, though at times he had jerked fretfully. Her touch on his shoulder seemed to calm him. When he fell still again, she watched his chest anxiously for movement. His breathing appeared to be more labored than when she'd first found him.

As the volume of the siren increased, it almost drowned out the sound of speeding footfalls in the barn.

"Grace?"

"In here!"

She sighed in relief when Aaron Raber, his bowl-cut hair tousled from where he jerked his hat off, poked his head and a shoulder through the small door.

"Gabe is almost here. On his way back from the shack, James flagged Ben down as he was passing. Ben told him to go back and call my business cell. Thankfully, I was working nearby. James also called others, who are on their way." While he was talking, Aaron scanned the silo's interior. His lips compressed as he saw the ladder ended several feet above the corn. But when he glanced back to Grace, he gave her a wink and a smile. "We'll get him out. Peter might not like the looks of his barn by the time we do, but we'll get him out. How's he doing?"

"He hasn't woken up yet, but he's breathing. But not so well anymore." Grace bit into her lower lip so deeply she tasted blood. "Aaron, I didn't think I'd be so long. I left the girls in the house…"

"I'm sure they're fine. But Rachel and the twins were with Ben. I'll send them into the house. Malinda and Fannie will be so busy with them, they won't even notice you've been longer than you expected."

Grace almost whimpered when he disappeared

again. The sound of the siren, after increasing in volume, abruptly stopped. More footfalls reverberated in the barn, along with fretful neighs and heavy foot stomping by the draft horses. A short moment later, Gabe, the local EMT, stuck his head in.

"Hi, Grace. How are you doing?" His face and voice were calm as he took in the situation.

When Grace's face contorted as she tried to control her tears, he apparently had his answer. "Well, I'll tell you, I think you've done very well indeed. You've got him uncovered, so we won't have to delay any longer in doing that. I understand that he's breathing, but he's not regained consciousness." At her nod, he continued. "Was he ever not breathing? Was he completely buried?"

"I don't think so. His face was visible when I found him."

"Good. Has he moved?"

"Only fretfully a few times."

"Have you moved him?" Gabe nodded in response to her rapid denial. "Good job. We'll stabilize him in case there were any injuries in the fall. I'm going to get in to you to take care of him. Peter won't like it, but we're going to have to take some of this wall down to get him out, so it's going to take a bit."

Chin quivering, Grace nodded.

"All right. I'll get to you as quickly as I can." Gabe ducked out of view.

Grace took her first full breath since the corn had come down. She pressed her lips together as she stared down at Peter's still face. Lifting a hand, she tenderly brushed his bangs from his forehead before cupping his cheek in her palm. "Just a little bit longer," she murmured. "Hang on just a little bit longer."

Though it surely wasn't that long, it felt like an hour or more before Grace heard a scrape and rattle above her. She looked up to see a blue-trousered leg, then two, followed by Ben Raber's full form emerging on the metal ladder overhead.

He gave her a nod. "I know it seems slow, but we need to make sure you don't have more of us falling down on you. So we need to make sure we can get to you safely. Don't worry, our volunteer fire department prepares for this. You two still doing all right?"

"Ja." Her voice quavered, almost making it a question.

"Gut." As Ben moved farther into the bin, she could see he wore a harness of some sort. Bits of grain and accompanying dust drizzled down as he worked overhead, securing a line to features of the silo that even to her looked more secure than the old rickety ladder.

Grace jerked when Peter coughed beside her. She bent over his face to protect it from debris from above. When she looked up again at the renewed commotion overhead, Gabe was working his way down the ladder with a black backpack in hand. He was wearing a harness with a sleek rope trailing from it that Ben played out as the EMT descended. Gabe reached the end of the ladder. Grace held her breath as he shifted from it to rappel down the last ten-foot stretch of wall with Ben bracing him from above.

As soon as his feet touched bottom, Gabe crossed to her, treading carefully to avoid disturbing the corn. Even so, the grain shifted slightly beneath Peter as he approached. When Grace's face contorted as he knelt beside her, Gabe gave her shoulder a reassuring squeeze.

"You're doing great. He's fortunate to have had you here." Gabe unzipped his backpack. The rope from overhead still dangled above him like a puppet string. "Now let's get some details on how Peter is doing."

Chapter Fifteen

Grace peeked in through the partially open bed-room door. She chewed on the tip of her finger, one she'd gnawed on fifteen minutes earlier when she'd checked in to see that the man on the bed still hadn't moved.

At the sound of footfalls, she ducked back into the hallway.

"Any changes?"

"*Nee*, Gabe. And it's been several hours since he fell."

The EMT frowned. "I certainly would have preferred that he go to the hospital to be checked out. But when he briefly came to in the silo and adamantly refused…" He shook his head. "I can't make them go." He sighed. "I checked him out as best I could when I cleaned him up. The cut on his head should be fine with the butterfly ban-dage, although he may have a headache for a bit. His limbs were all moving fine when he was awake, although again, I really would've rather he had some X-rays to be sure. The cough bothers me too. He could hardly get a word around it when he woke up. Does he have issues with asthma?"

"I don't know." Grace crossed her arms over her chest, aware that there was so much she didn't know about Peter. Only that she loved him and was worried about him. Something that was now surely evident to all and sundry, as she had barely left his side in the silo, only enough to make room for the men while they were working to free him.

"Even if he hadn't before, grain dust can cause or certainly aggravate it. How are you doing? Any issues from the dust?"

Grace shook her head. "Not since we got out of the silo."

The EMT glanced at his watch. "I wish I could stay longer. Are you sure you'll be all right?" He tilted his head in the direction of the bedroom.

"*Ja.* I'll be here anyway for the girls. I'll let you know as soon as he wakes up."

Gabe rubbed a hand over his jaw. "How close is your nearest phone shack?"

"I think I can help out there."

Gabe and Grace glanced toward the end of the hall. At the sight of Gideon, they quietly headed in his direction. Gideon had come out this morning, along with every other employee of Schrock Brothers' Furniture, as the business had closed for the day to assist getting Peter out of the silo.

They, and other men from the community, had taken care of the barn's livestock after removing a section of the wall to free Peter. Once he was out, they'd all stayed to clean up spilled corn and rebuild the wall.

As soon as Peter was freed from the silo, Grace had hurried into the house to wash the corn dust off before she joined Rachel Raber, Ben's wife, who was already preparing food for the workers. Other buggies of men and women had arrived throughout the day to assist in whatever way they could. But at this hour, as there was nothing else to be done except wait for Peter to awaken, they'd gone home to do their own chores.

Gideon held up a cell phone. Gabe smiled at the sight.

"Call me when he wakes up. And see if you can convince him to see a doctor tomorrow."

Grace nodded. "I'll try. But I don't promise anything on the doctor." Gabe grimaced in acknowledgment. With a two-fingered wave, he headed out.

Gideon followed Grace into the common room. "One of the reasons I'm not in a hurry to end my *rumspringa*," Gideon joked as he showed her how to use the phone and set up Gabe's number so it was easy to find. "This way, at least until Peter's out of the woods, you don't have to worry about getting to the phone shack. But—" he rolled his eyes "—if it's not Gabe calling to check, or one of the men's names, you might not want to answer it."

Grace couldn't prevent a smile. "You mean the girls who call might be unhappy if I answer."

Gideon's grin was slow and revealed a charming amount of white teeth. "They might be a bit surprised. Probably best if you don't read the texts either."

Her eyes rounded. "Are you sure you want to loan it?"

"*Ja*. Consider it a recess for me, teacher."

After the stress of the day, it felt good to giggle. Grace tentatively scrolled through the contacts as he'd just shown her, raising her eyebrows at all the female names. "For sure and certain, there are a lot of them in here. I didn't know this many girls had phones in their *rumspringa*."

She pressed the phone to her chest and clasped both hands over it. "*Denki*, Gideon. I'll take *gut* care of it and get it back to you, hopefully soon. I'm sure Peter appreciates it too."

"He probably won't, by the time I'm finished." With those odd words, Gideon took his leave as well.

Grace followed him to the door and returned his jaunty wave as he drove out of the lane. She frowned at the phone in her hand, the one with several names of girls who would like to attract this man. Why wasn't she one of them? Why, for her, was it the unattainable, more solemn man inside instead of this charming bachelor? Shaking her head, Grace returned to the house.

Peter groaned. The way his chest felt, he was prepared to open his eyes to see Bella standing on it with all four hooves. Each exhale sounded like the wheeze of a bellows. His head ached. He touched a hand to it only to brush his fingers against wadded gauze instead of the skin he'd expected.

Opening his eyes, he discovered he was not in the *daadi haus*, but in his downstairs bedroom in the main house. What had happened?

He jerked upright, setting off a spasm of coughing. The silo. The corn. Falling. Grace. Was she all right? Had it buried her when it came down? Panting in between coughs, he struggled with the blankets as he tried to work his legs to the edge of the bed.

Lightheaded from his efforts, Peter dropped back against the pillow to catch his breath. It felt like a cinch was being tightened around his chest. Asthma. He recognized the signs. He'd been such a fool. He knew his problem with grain dust, and he'd gone in anyway without a mask. He also knew better than to enter a silo by himself. He was a volunteer firefighter. He was aware of the dangers. But he'd forgotten all that in the mess he'd created for himself over a woman.

And Grace had been there, leaning through the small doorway, when the ladder shifted beneath him and everything had come tumbling down. Had she been buried in the deluge? Struck by the ladder? If he hurt her, he'd never forgive himself. Peter pressed a hand to his chest against the breathlessness as he tried to rise.

When the door swung open, he sagged back onto the bed. "You're all right," he wheezed as Grace peeked in.

"Ja." He sucked in a breath at the smile that lit her face, setting himself off in another fit of coughing. She hurried into the room. "But you're not. And you should be staying in bed."

For the moment, swamped by relief at seeing her and void of energy, Peter couldn't disagree. He let her tuck in the covers at his side. When she saw he wasn't going to lie down again, she arranged the pillows more comfortably at his back.

"Why am I in here and not the *daadi haus*?"

"It's easier to hear you if you're in this part of the house."

"The girls? Are the girls all right?"

"They're fine. They've gone to bed. They've been in to see you sleeping before they went. I can wake them if you like, or have them see you first thing in the morning."

"Let them sleep. It's that late?" He looked about the room. Only now did he realize it was lit by lamplight.

"*Ja.* You were out all day. Gabe and everyone else were worried about you. You woke up long enough while you were still in the silo to tell Gabe you didn't want to go to the hospital. He was quite concerned about that. But you…you're stubborn even when not in control of all your senses." Grace stepped back from the bed and crossed her arms over her chest. "He was worried about possible head and spinal injuries, but he said he couldn't make you go to the hospital, so he checked you out as best he could. He said someone needed to stay with you for a few days." Even by lamplight, he could see her cheeks were a bit rosy. "I was the most likely candidate since I was already here."

Peter met her uncertain gaze. He remembered now. How could he forget? She'd said she was going to go home to her little house. He'd almost collapsed with relief when she'd said she was coming back in the morning. He ran his tongue over his lips, tasting corn dust. "At least you get hot water here."

He was rewarded with another smile. "About the only benefit. That and the girls." Their gazes locked. And held. Her throat bobbed in a swallow before she looked down to smooth a hand over her apron. "Now that you're awake, do you need anything? I'm to allow you some water and possibly something for the pain. After that, we'll see. Gabe finally left around suppertime. And you're to call him now that you're awake."

Peter twisted his lips. "That's all well and good, but I think it will still be just a bit before I can make it to the phone shack."

"Oh, that's not a problem. Gideon gave me his cell phone to use."

Peter jerked his head up so fast he banged it on the headboard. He narrowed his eyes against the pain, both in his head and his heart, at that bit of information. "Did he? That was…neighborly of him."

Grace leaned down to pick up the device—one Peter hadn't noticed—from the nightstand and pressed a few buttons on it. "Here." The phone was already ringing when she handed it to him. "I'll get you some water and be right back."

Peter scowled at the phone. Even when he'd been in his *rumspringa*, he hadn't had one. He certainly didn't want to use *this* one. But when he heard Gabe's voice on the line, he put it to his ear. By the time Grace was back with a glass of water, he'd filled the EMT in on how he was feeling. And listened to gentle chiding on his resistance to go to the hospital.

Having ended the call, Peter put the phone in

the drawer of the nightstand. "I managed to assure him that I'll at least live until tomorrow." Even to him, the statement lacked conviction when it ended in a coughing fit. Grace set the glass on the nightstand until he was in control enough to pick it up. He drank thirstily, washing what felt like an acre of dust down his throat.

Relieved to discover Gabe had clothed him before putting him in bed, Peter set the glass on the nightstand and flipped the covers back. Gritting his teeth, he swung his legs to the edge of the mattress. "I'm going to check my livestock."

Grace's jaw dropped. "You need to stay in bed. You just woke up after being out most of the day."

"I'm going to check my livestock. You can be a help." He scowled at where she stood between him and the door. "Or hindrance."

She heaved a sigh. "Since I won't be able to drag you back into the house should you fall, I might as well go along to try to keep you upright." With a glare in his direction, she jerked the nightstand drawer open and retrieved the cell phone. "But I won't help unless you can get out of bed by yourself."

"I will," Peter bit out, although he was sweating by the time he managed to do so. When finally upright, he shot her a grin, weak but triumphant.

"That's all well and good," Grace admitted

with a slight smile of her own. "But how will you be when you let go of the headboard?"

When he wobbled after doing so, she rolled her eyes. "Gabe will think I'm a terrible caretaker," she muttered as she reached out an arm to support him.

"I think you're a *wunderbar* one." Peter clasped a hand around it, unable to distinguish whether his rapid heartbeat was due to his efforts or the feel of her lithe, strong elbow under the material of her dress. Though the physical distance was close between them, he needed to maintain the mental one. He cleared his throat. "And I'm the one who employs you, not him." Peter cringed inwardly when the slender arm in his gentle grasp stiffened.

They shuffled to the door. When he had to lean on the doorjamb a moment upon reaching it, Grace furrowed her brow. "Are you sure about this? The men did the chores before they left. They would have taken good care of your livestock."

Peter pushed away from the doorway. "I want to look in on my animals. They are my responsibility." He pressed his lips together, uncomfortable in sharing that seeing his livestock, being with them, would give him a sense of peace and stability that he fiercely needed, as his world currently felt out of control. Regardless of what he'd told Gabe, he was as weak and wobbly as a new-born foal. Even so, he was glad he had regained consciousness enough to keep from going to the hospital. He hardly had money enough to pay Grace, much less a hospital bill. The community would cover what he couldn't, but he was already such a sorry figure in the district—the man who couldn't keep his own wife—that he didn't need them paying his bills as well.

The full moon illuminated their trip across the farmyard. At their creeping pace, Peter grimly wondered if they'd be able to return to the house before sunrise. Halfway to the barn, he was besieged by a coughing fit that had him doubled over.

"You stubborn, foolish man," Grace murmured as she looped his arm over her shoulder when he finally straightened after wheezing to a stop. Peter could hear the worry underlying her voice. "I'll fix up a stall for you next to one of your precious animals." They lurched onward.

"You might have to." Peter squeezed his eyes shut. Did his lightheadedness come from the coughing? Or the feel of Grace nestled under his arm and along his side? He feared it was the latter. He leaned against the barn wall as she opened the door and went to light a lantern before returning to assist him inside. Once there, amongst the comforting scents and sounds of the animals, who stirred quietly at the unusually late visit, he sagged onto a hay bale. Bracing his hands behind him, Peter scanned the stalls' occupants.

Grace went to light another lantern, further illuminating the curious heads that hung over the stall doors. "Everyone present and accounted for."

"Looks like we even have a new face." Peter nodded toward the pony, which appeared in miniature in her stall next to the big draft horses.

"Ja." Grace's lips curved in a smile as she crossed to the little mare and began petting the pony's neck. "James brought her over just after you and the corn came down. He was the one to race to the phone shack and call for help." She stopped in mid stroke, looking stricken. "I forgot to pay him for Sunny."

"I'm sure he knows you're good for it."

"I'll make sure to pay him tomorrow."

Peter cocked his head in question.

"He's going to be doing chores while you're laid up. At least the ones the girls and I can't do."

Peter inhaled sharply and opened his mouth to argue, only to, aggravated by the barn dust, be unable to wheeze out the words. His head lolled between his shoulders. He nodded slowly. When he thought he had the breath to do so, he pushed to his feet and shambled over to Bella's stall. The big mare almost knocked him over when she rubbed her head against him. Peter curled his fingers over the stall wall to keep from staggering back. He searched the stall for the colt, finally spying the foal partially hidden in the shadows from where he peeked around behind his mother. Still, Peter could see the youngster looked alert and robust.

He rubbed the big mare's muscular neck. "*Gut* job, mama." He shuffled around to lean against the stall's half wall and crossed his arms over his chest as he examined the back wall of his barn.

"They had to take down part of where the silo adjoined to get you out. It took a while." Peter could read in Grace's face that it had been a long while indeed.

"My neighbors did a *gut* job."

"The corn that spilled is in a wagon behind the barn. It's not supposed to rain for a few days, so they figured it was all right there until you determine what you want to do with it."

Peter nodded. Grace was across the center aisle of the barn, fiddling with the pony's mane, stroking her fingers through it, unraveling the tangles as she did so. He sighed. Too bad she couldn't unravel the tangles in his life. It felt so…*right* with her in the barn. Maybe it was his current physical weakness, but watching her, Peter was as close to tears, to succumbing to despair, as he ever remembered being. Even in those dark, dark days both before *and* after Lucetta left.

Why was it more painful seeing what could have been instead of dealing with what was? He and Grace could have fit so well together. As partners, as parents, as husband and wife. He smiled ruefully. Her with her pony, him with his huge horses. Whatever children they would've had would have been happy and confident, secure in a lifetime of love.

Had his girls been emotionally damaged in their years with Lucetta? He knew he was. Damaged and hopelessly trapped. Tightness crushed his chest. Asthma? Or his situation?

Maybe it was the serenity of the barn in the lamplight. Maybe it was his own physical weakness. Maybe it was the peace that came to him here with his livestock. The peace that, even with the hopelessness of his situation, made him honest.

"It will never work, Grace," he said quietly.

She went still at his words. The pony nickered. After a moment, her head still bowed over the mare, Grace gave a final stroke to the mare's forelock before she straightened and turned in his direction. "You ready to go back?"

Back to the hopelessness and distrust before he got to know her? Peter twisted his lips and nodded somberly. Grace brushed her hands together. Wiping off dust from the pony? Or brushing away the attraction he knew she felt for him? She'd be better if it was the latter.

Peter made every effort to cross the yard under his own power. He knew his face was white with the effort. He had almost made it before slumping under a fit of coughing ten feet from the house. Without a word, Grace again ducked under his arm to support him. But Peter could feel the difference. Now, even with their physical closeness, there was a distance that hadn't been there on the trip to the barn.

Chapter Sixteen

Grace tucked Gideon's phone into the little interior pocket she'd sewn in the waistband of her dress. She'd return it to him today at church. Her hand tightened on the device briefly as she recalled how reluctantly Peter had accepted it and how he couldn't put it out of sight in a drawer fast enough. Her nose prickled, threatening tears.

Much like he had done with her.

In the few days since the silo incident, Peter had managed without her help. Fine caretaker she was. Of course, it was difficult to be a caretaker when your patient kept you at arm's length. Or rather, room's length. Malinda and Fannie had been more than happy to lend their assistance, fetching and carrying for their *daed*, and he was more than happy to let them.

Gabe had come by daily. Though he admitted their patient was on the mend, they were both relieved when Peter conceded to visit a doctor. From the look on his face when he emerged from the office, he hadn't been happy about the appointment. But she was growing used to his cloudy countenance. Flowers may be blooming outside and their part of Wisconsin might have warmer temperatures, but it was definitely winter, at least when the wind blew in her direction, inside the Lehman farmhouse.

It was winter in her heart as well.

It will never work, Grace.

Grace winced. Peter wouldn't have said the words if he hadn't known how she felt about him. If he hadn't been aware of her longings for him and unrealistic but apparently transparent dreams for the future. Had she given him some clue as to what the feel of his arm about her shoulders did to her as she'd helped him to the barn?

When she let herself stop to think about it, Grace was almost nauseous with humiliation. Why did she repeatedly fall for men who weren't interested or were ultimately unavailable? She'd been embarrassed by the situation with Willis. But it had stopped at embarrassment. Once she left Iowa, that embarrassment had quickly migrated to relief at being out of that situation.

With Peter... *Oh, Peter!* Grace sniffed. In time, she might get over the embarrassment that he'd discovered her feelings for him. But the heartache of loving him? She was afraid it would be her close companion for years to come. Even if she grew to love someone else, she feared every sight of Peter and the girls over the years—the girls growing up without a mother and Peter growing older and more solitary—would crack and peel away another bit of her heart.

Grace's lips twisted. She'd probably see him more in the community later than she was seeing him now under the same roof. The girls carried his meals in to him, sometimes joining him there while he ate, before carrying the plates back. If *she* peeked into the room, he was fine, perfectly fine. Didn't need anything at all. At least according to him.

According to the doctor, he needed a little device to help him breathe when the coughing got really bad, currently a common occurrence at night. Which is why she hadn't gone back to her little rental yet. She would sit up in bed, listening to Peter coughing so hard in his room downstairs that it was a wonder he could take in any air at all.

The first night, she'd come flying down the steps to check on him. Even in the dim lamplight, it was visible enough to read his glare that warned her to retreat upstairs without stepping a foot inside the door. She crept back up and tried not to feel sorry for Peter when he looked like a wreck in the morning.

As he did today, which was the reason he wasn't going to church with her and the girls. Grace had suggested staying home with him, but

Peter wouldn't hear of it. Weak as he still was, he practically shoved her and the girls out the door even before Aaron and Miriam stopped by to pick them up.

Grace impatiently brushed away a tear that leaked down her cheek. Peter didn't want her. For anything except for caring for his daughters. He'd made that perfectly clear. She drew in a long breath. That's all he'd hired her for. She was the one who'd forgotten her limited role. A mistake that had apparently prompted Peter to push her at other men.

Grace patted the little pocket to ensure Gideon's phone was safe. She would return it to him today. And if Gideon or any other man—available man—in the community expressed an interest in her, maybe it was time she returned that as well.

Peter drummed his fingers on the arm of his lounge chair. He picked up a farm magazine, flipped through a few pages and dropped it back down on the end table. Craning his neck to the side, he could see the clock in the kitchen. It was five minutes later than the last time he'd looked.

Why weren't they back yet? It was late afternoon. Surely Miriam and Aaron would've had enough time to visit by now and bring his family—correction—his girls, home.

Along with Grace.

Maybe he should have let her stay with him today. Even if he didn't interact with her, as long as she was in some part of the house, it wouldn't feel so empty. Like other things in his life. With his finger, Peter flicked the magazine away from the inhaler he'd inadvertently covered up. The one prescribed by the doctor who'd told him, well meaning of course, that with his "occupational asthma," induced by grain dust and other likely irritants, including animal dander, maybe he should think of another career.

Peter had come out of the crammed little examination room thinking maybe he should think of another doctor. But the past few rough nights, and sometimes during the day, had him wondering if another doctor would tell him the same thing.

What if he could no longer farm?

His fingers curled tightly around the ends of the armrests until the wood threatened to crack. No Grace. No farming. No joy, except for his girls. Peter squeezed his eyes shut. No hope.

He smiled grimly. He always figured if anything kept him from making a go of the farm, it would be money. And he would battle that as long and as hard as he could with relentless work. He never imagined his health might put an end to his dream of making a success of his own place.

For sure and certain, he could sell it. With large families in a restricted geographic area, farmland was always in demand. He'd heard of some Amish men asking the descendants of *Englisch* neighbors who'd passed away about selling the land, almost before the funerals were held. Certainly not a way to facilitate happy relationships in the neighborhood.

Ja. He could easily sell the farm. But he went numb at the prospect of doing so.

If he did sell, what would he do? Stay in Miller's Creek and work for someone else? Carpentry? It had dust. Dairies? Dust. Furniture making? Sawmills? All had irritants. He grimaced. If he went home to Kentucky, it would be the same thing. The work there was mainly farming. He would be doing it for someone else instead of working for himself.

His head slumped against the back of the lounge chair. At least he'd have childcare in Kentucky. He wouldn't have to see Grace. To wonder what she was doing. To watch her with the fortunate man she would choose as a partner. Maybe that would be a *gut* thing.

Where was she? Peter craned his neck to check the kitchen wall clock again. At the sound of a buggy turning into the lane, he jerked upright. *Finally.*

He was flipping through the *Budget*—like

he hadn't read through it twice already—when the front door opened. He casually looked up as Malinda, Miriam carrying her toddler son, and Aaron with a droopy-eyed Fannie entered the common room. Peter's gaze flicked back to the doorway, but no one else came in. He furrowed his brow before nodding at the arrivals.

"*Denki* for taking them." He smiled as Aaron carefully set Fannie down in a padded rocking chair. "Looks like she wore herself out."

Aaron straightened and relieved Miriam of their son. She pressed a hand on her rounded torso and arched her back. "They were certainly busy playing. You were missed at church today. Everyone was wondering how you were doing."

"It's been slower than I would have hoped." Peter's smile faded as he added solemnly, "I can't thank the community enough for their help. I feel so foolish." Peter rubbed his hand across the back of his neck. "I knew better than to do what I did."

Aaron grinned. "You aren't the first to make a mistake. And you won't be the last."

Miriam patted her husband's shoulder. "And he ought to know."

Aaron rolled his eyes. "Regrettably, she's right." He leaned his cheek against the little one slumped against his shoulder. "Speaking of worn out, this one is as well. Before we go, do you want me to do your chores?"

Chagrined that he couldn't even do his own chores, Peter cautiously drew in a long inhalation, wary in case it set him off in a fit of coughing. "*Nee.* James Yoder has been taking care of those until I'm more up and around. I can't pay him, but in return for the chores and some fieldwork, I promised him the dairy calf my cow will later have."

"Is there anything else we can do for you while we're here?" When Peter shook his head, Miriam continued, "Then I guess we'll be going."

Peter glanced toward the door. "Did you forget someone?"

Miriam and Aaron regarded each other with arched eyebrows.

"Where's Grace?" Peter blurted. Heat crept up his cheeks.

"Oh." Miriam's response was more drawn out than the simple word deserved. And what did that look in her eye mean? "She stayed to go to the Singing tonight."

Peter scowled. "How's she going to get home?"

Miriam smiled. "I'm sure she'll find a ride. From the young men flocking around her this afternoon, I don't think that will be a problem."

The news should have delighted him. After all, he'd set it in motion. It didn't. Miriam must have read his face as surely as if he was the *Budget*.

"I thought that was the purpose of your visits

with the single men of the district. To find Grace a beau."

His scowl deepened. "Does nothing stay private in this community?"

"Was that your intention? You didn't succeed. It spread like a grass fire in a drought."

Peter crossed his arms over his chest. Miriam didn't have to look so pleased about it. "I only talked to two people."

"*Ach*, a lot more heard than that. At the way things looked though, we'll be searching for a new schoolteacher come fall."

The words were like a kick to his stomach. Women couldn't teach if they were married. It was assumed they would be busy taking care of their families. It was what he wanted, wasn't it? For Grace, though physically close while she worked for him, to be emotionally unattainable? If so, why did despair claw at him like a starving dog gnawing on a juicy bone?

Peter forced a swallow. "A gain for her new husband but a loss for the district, as she seems like she's a *gut* teacher. I'll make sure she gets in all right tonight." He shifted uncomfortably under Miriam's steady gaze. Before heading out the door, she gave him a sympathetic smile.

"A loss indeed, Peter."

Chapter Seventeen

Grace sighed in relief when no lamplight glow was visible from either the windows of the common room or Peter's bedroom. *And why would you think he would still be up just because you're out late? He never stays up even when it's early and you're in the house.*

"Tired?" Her companion sent her a lazy smile.

"Not of your company." Was that too flirtatious? It had been so long since someone had brought her home from a Singing. Grace crossed her arms over her chest, hugging herself as she accepted the truth of her statement. Gideon was *wunderbar* company. Attentive, charming, cheerfully steady in nature. Unlike someone else she knew. Gideon just wasn't…the someone else she knew.

Unsure of her responsibilities as hostess since it wasn't actually her home, and uncertain of his intentions should she stay in the buggy once he pulled up to the hitching post, Grace scrambled down as soon as Gideon drew the Standardbred to a stop. She swallowed when he climbed down as well. Apparently his intentions were to come inside. Which was no surprise. During courting, many a young man brought a girl home to her family and stayed until the wee hours of the morning as the couple got to know each other.

Was he courting her? Casting a wary glance in his direction, Grace hastened up the sidewalk. She'd been relieved, flattered and a little embarrassed when Gideon had sought her out and asked to drive her home from tonight's Singing. Relieved, as she then didn't have to secure another way back with a girlfriend or the girl's brother. Flattered, as Gideon, who was not a frequent attendant of Sunday night Singings, to the dismay of local girls, was a much sought after companion. And embarrassed. Those surreptitiously watching as Gideon helped her into his buggy were surely wondering—as was she—if he was asking only because of Peter's ridiculous campaign to find her a beau. Her ears burned at the knowledge that everyone in the district seemed to know of Peter's efforts.

Grace worried her lower lip as she entered the house, with Gideon following a few steps behind. Should she offer him some refreshments? Stay in the common room with its more comfortable furniture? Or direct him to the kitchen? The latter was a better choice, as it was farthest from

Peter's bedroom. She certainly didn't want to disturb him. The thought of Peter's nearness when there was another man in the house was disturbing enough for her.

She was crossing to the kitchen when a voice called out of the darkness.

"It's about time you got home."

Grace jumped, bumping back into Gideon's broad chest. She peered wide-eyed into the shadows of the room until, her vision growing accustomed to the darkness, she could pick out Peter's form in his chair.

"What are you doing up?" Her question was more squeak than voice.

Peter lit the lamp beside him to reveal his unsmiling face. "As folks seem to think I'm not capable of doing my own chores, I don't have to get up as early in the morning. Lets me stay up a little later and see what my…employee is doing."

Grace's brow furrowed at his tone and emphasis. She'd spent many solitary hours in this room after Peter's early disappearances to the *daadi haus*. "I've been in the house in the evenings for some time. It never seemed to bother you then what I was doing at night."

"I assumed you were taking care of my daughters."

Grace glanced, searching for any dark shapes

that might be the girls curled up on the chairs or couch.

"I put them to bed. I've done it many times before. Besides, their caretaker was missing."

Grace hissed in a breath. With the excitement of attending the Singing that evening, she'd forgotten about bedtime rituals with Malinda and Fannie. She glanced toward the door to the stairway. Had they settled down all right? She felt the weight of Peter's gaze from across the room. Pressing her lips together, Grace stared back at his shadowed form. She wouldn't always be here. Soon she'd be going back to her little house. As he said, he'd put the girls to bed many times before. She refused to feel guilty. Until Peter started coughing.

"You should be in bed yourself."

"I'm heading there," he wheezed. "I just wanted to make sure you got home all right."

Her guilt elevated. "As you can see, I'm fine." A glance at Gideon found a smile aimed in her direction, one Grace was relieved to return in small measure. "Gideon saved me from having to beg a ride home."

"Happy to do so." Her companion's smile widened. "And I doubt any begging would've been necessary. I was just glad I was first in line to ask."

Heat crept up Grace's cheeks at the reminder

of Peter's scheme to find her a beau. Guilt fled as embarrassment took residence. Peter's scowl, when she looked back in his direction, suggested that if Gideon was happy with the evening's events, he was the only one in the room to be so. Contrarily, the prospect made Grace feel a little better.

"Aren't you glad your efforts worked so well?" The smile she tossed across the room to Peter before escaping into the kitchen was a mite too sweet to be sincere.

The mundane tasks of making lemonade and preparing a tray of cookies helped her regain her composure. She took a deep breath and returned with the refreshments to the common room to find Gideon alone. When her shoulders slumped, Grace didn't stop to examine if it was prompted by relief or disappointment.

Gideon winked at her as she set the tray down on the end table between them. Just as she was lowering herself onto the rocker, a call came from down the hall. Though not loud enough to wake the girls upstairs, it was definitely loud enough to make her jolt, especially as she'd never heard its like before.

"Grace!"

Straightening, she sent a puzzled glance toward Gideon before heading down the hall to Peter's room. She stopped at the doorway to glance into the room.

"I need a glass of water." He glowered at her from the bed. "Please."

Grace propped her hands on her hips. Since the silo incident, Peter never asked for anything. At least not from her. Shaking her head, she went to the kitchen and returned a minute later with a half-full glass. She set it on the nightstand at the same time Peter reached for it. His fingers brushed the back of her hand. They both froze. Her sharp inhalation echoed his. Still gripping the glass, Grace nudged it forward a fraction and carefully withdrew her hand in the created space. Avoiding eye contact, she pivoted and fled the room.

She burst into the common room, momentarily surprised to find Gideon there before she recalled he'd given her a ride home. He raised an eyebrow at her expression before smiling and setting down the farm magazine he'd been flipping through as she dropped into the rocker.

"Grace!"

She remained seated, her brows lowered, her mouth compressed, as Gideon's smile turned into a smirk.

Grace's heartbeat hadn't yet slowed from her last visit to Peter's room. She wasn't sure she could handle another trip so soon. What could he want? Surely not to discuss that...that moment. She knew what *she* wanted to discuss. His odd behavior.

"It isn't funny. He's normally not like this. He never asks for help. I don't know what's wrong with him, I mean, other than his coughing fits."

Gideon rubbed a hand across his mouth. "I do."

With a bracing breath and an apologetic smile, Grace pushed to her feet. "I need to see what he wants."

"You do that. But I doubt he'll tell you."

Frowning at Gideon's words, Grace retraced her steps down the hall to Peter's bedroom and peeked in. *"Ja?"*

Peter didn't look up, just kept plucking at the well-worn quilt that covered his chest. "Would you open the window?"

Grace was glad the width of the room was between them as she crossed it. She could understand his request. It was a pleasant night out, or at least it had been before she came into the house. But this was something Peter could have done before he climbed into bed. Something he *would* have done on his own any other night. Aware of his hooded gaze, she opened the window a few inches and quickly retreated to the common room.

With a fixed smile, Grace smoothed her skirt as she sat down in the rocker. Gideon met it with one of his own as he brushed cookie crumbs from his hands. "You're a *gut* cook. Peter was certainly right about that."

Grace's smile faltered. "I am so sorry. And so embarrassed. I never imagined he would...would hawk me like I was something at the annual mud sale." Her eyes widened. "I hope you don't think I put him up to it."

"*Nee*. I'm sure Peter came up with the idea himself. And for his own reasons. You don't need someone to advertise for you. You're a pretty *gut* advertisement yourself, Grace. I'm just glad—"

"Grace!" The call echoed down the narrow hallway.

Her *kapp* crinkled against her hair as Grace pressed her head against the back of the rocker. Regardless of her current confusion and erratic heart rate, the other evening Peter had been plenty straightforward. *It will never work, Grace.* The quiet words still rang in her ears. They continually echoed, as she knew in her heart his words were true. They'd also been followed by days of Peter avoiding her. He had made sure she knew he didn't want her. The man had even been soliciting dates on her behalf.

Tonight, when she was courted by a beau *he'd personally contacted about her*, Peter seemed reluctant to let her out of his sight.

He couldn't have it both ways. As much as she

wanted to respond to him, her tattered emotions dictated she shouldn't. At least Willis, when he'd cast her off, had made it permanent. Or as permanent as could be until Cora was killed and their mothers got involved again. Besides, she'd made the decision this morning to return the interest of other men—eligible men—in the community. Hadn't she? She gritted her teeth. If she hadn't, she should.

Grace glanced wryly at Gideon. Bracing her hands on the rocker's wooden arms, she lunged to her feet, leaving the chair creaking in motion behind her as she stomped down the hallway.

She stepped a few feet into the bedroom and folded her arms over her chest. "What is it?"

This time, Peter looked up from the bed. His mouth hooked down at her stiff position. He folded his own leanly muscled arms over his faded pajama shirt. "I need another blanket."

"How about I just close the window you had me open five minutes ago," she retorted.

He tightened his jaw. "No, I want it open."

"I'm glad you know something you want. You want others to walk out with me. Except when they actually try doing so, then you don't want them to. I think you're just being a dog in a manger. Not wanting someone else to have what's of no use to you."

The strong column of Peter's throat bobbed

in a hard swallow. He opened his mouth, only to close it again with the click of his teeth.

At the whisper of movement in the hallway, Grace looked back to find Gideon behind her, propping a relaxed shoulder against the doorjamb. Discomfited to have a witness to Peter and her…discussion, Grace ducked past Gideon to the main floor's other bedroom and stripped the two blankets off the bed. Gideon stepped back out of the way as she struggled to get her large bundle through the door. Once she did, she stalked across the room to drop them into Peter's lap, almost burying him.

Gideon's eyes glinted with laughter. "I've got work tomorrow. I don't know why it's called Schrock Brothers, as Malachi makes the decisions and I just make furniture, but he likes me to set a *gut* example by not showing up late. So I guess I better be leaving. I enjoyed bringing you home tonight, Grace. We'll do it again sometime." He flicked a glance toward Peter. "Maybe with fewer interruptions."

Grace schooled her expression at Gideon's words. She certainly enjoyed Gideon's company. He made her feel interesting. Attractive. A refreshing change from Peter, who, right now, had her so confused she didn't know what to think. Confused…and unsuitably energized.

"I'll see you out."

"Probably better not." Gideon inclined his head toward Peter, who had shoved the blankets to the side. "If you do, he might find a reason for me to check on the livestock or milk the cow."

"If he suggests it, I'll go out and do it. Right now, I'd prefer their company to his." Grace looked at Peter over her shoulder. "If there's nothing else, I'm going upstairs." Before he could answer, she slipped past a grinning Gideon and headed down the hallway.

She did see Gideon to the door and waved as his buggy rumbled down the lane before returning to the common room where she turned out the lamps. All the while, she listened for any sounds from the downstairs bedrooms. There was only silence. She finally headed upstairs.

It will never work, Grace.

She opened her own window and leaned her elbows on the sill, hoping the night sounds would soothe or at least distract her. She knew he was right. Knew her feelings for Peter were wrong.

Then why couldn't she stop loving him?

It was a long time before she slept.

Chapter Eighteen

"See you later. I'll be back for evening chores." James pushed off on his scooter to send it barreling down the lane.

Peter, settling onto the seat of the hay mower, waved at the departing youth. He had to admit James had been a big help while he recovered from the silo incident. Although he was getting around much better, in closed spaces, dust could still prompt wheezing and chest tightness.

Fortunately, working outside wasn't such an issue. He gathered the lines and called to the team. "Walk on."

The mower lurched as the two Belgians headed for the field. Grace had given him a look when he'd stated he was mowing hay today. Peter knew she worried about him. But he knew he was well enough to cut his own hay. He was only sitting on the mower, the horses were doing all the work. He wasn't helpless. He didn't need to bother his neighbors. Again. The mowing needed to be done. He'd needed to get away from the house. And Grace.

Having reached the hayfield, Peter lined the Belgians up for the first pass. He kicked the lever with his heel to put the mower into gear, lowered the sickle bar and watched as the alfalfa began falling in a swath beside him.

It was time for Grace to leave.

He didn't need to bother the single neighbors again about walking out with her. Peter scowled. That hadn't been one of his better ideas. He'd thought if Grace belonged to someone else, it would provide a sense of emotional distance. Would help him rebuild his mental barriers to any foolish inclinations. Would keep him from loving her.

Peter swept his hat from his head and rubbed a rough hand through his hair. He'd thought wrong. Seeing Grace with Gideon a few nights ago had sliced him up as surely as the sickle bar was cutting through the alfalfa.

His pain didn't change the fact that it wouldn't work between them. No matter how he wished it was different, he was a married man. Peter was surprised the district hadn't raised a collective eyebrow that Grace had been staying at his home. He ought to be glad they trusted the two of them so much. But perhaps it was less trust and more that he was such a pathetic creature.

The man who couldn't hold on to his wife.

Peter's lips twitched. He couldn't have acted more pathetic than he had Sunday night when Gideon had brought Grace home from the Singing. Good thing the man was good-natured. Peter didn't know what he would have done had the situation been reversed. But it wouldn't have been with just a smile and shake of his head as he'd departed.

Monday morning, embarrassed by his prior evening's behavior and apprehensive about what Grace's response might be—deserved to be— he'd headed to the barn even before James arrived for chores. Following a breakfast filled as much with wary glances and one-word responses as with pancakes and sausage, he'd escaped to the garden, using the hoe more to lean on at times than to dig in the soil.

Later that morning, Grace and the girls had come out to help. By dinnertime, conversations had come easier. There'd even been moments when his gaze had collided with hers to catch her wearing a sad smile. Was it more sadness, or more smile? Had his behavior the previous evening upset, or amused her? Though not thrilled to be a source of amusement, it was much better than having upset her.

Which was why he'd been startled—and panicked—when Grace announced she was going home to her little house that evening. Had he driven her away? *Was she coming back?* His legs shaky, Peter had leaned on his hoe when she'd assured the girls—who'd asked the question with quivering chins—that she'd return in the morning.

He'd spent the night staring at the ceiling, wondering if she really would. Lucetta had done a *gut* job of teaching him not to trust a woman.

Peter absently lined the shoe of the mower up with the swath path as he started another trip around the field. Putting the girls to bed Monday night had been difficult. He'd done it numerous times by himself before, even the previous night. But then, the three of them had thought it was temporary, that Grace would be a consistent part of the nighttime ritual. In the relatively short time she'd been there, she'd made her mark.

"Grace reads us two books before bed," Malinda had lamented.

"Where's our song?" Fannie had charged.

There was more of "That's not how Grace did it" and "Grace did this." But it was the next question that made him freeze.

"*Daed*, why didn't you marry Grace instead of our *mamm*?"

His mouth had gone dry. "I didn't know Grace then, Fannie."

"Well, you should've waited to meet her before you got married."

He'd brushed a hand over his youngest daughter's hair. "I wouldn't have had you two then. And I can't imagine my life without you."

"Even though you're happier when you're with Grace?"

At Malinda's question, he'd tugged gently on the end of her braid. "Even then."

"We're happier with Grace."

He'd smiled sadly. "I know, Fannie."

"So why don't you marry her now?"

Peter remembered squeezing his eyes shut in regret. "I can't. I'm already married, Fannie. To your *mamm*."

"She's not coming back, is she?"

Hearing the apprehension in Malinda's voice, though he'd longed to reassure her, he'd hesitated. He didn't want to lie to his children. "It's...possible."

"Does she have to?" Malinda's whimper had been quickly joined by Fannie's wail.

"I want to keep Grace!"

As much as the prospect of Lucetta's return chilled Peter, his girls' reactions gutted him to the core.

"Nothing is going to change at the moment. But...your *mamm* and I are married. We made vows before *Gott*. As long as we are alive, she will always be my wife. If she comes back to the community, she's coming back to us."

"Oh, *Daadi*. Why didn't you marry someone like Grace instead?"

His daughter's cry still echoed in his head. Peter halted the horses and took the mower out of gear before stepping down to clear a jam of alfalfa from the blade. He couldn't explain to Malinda that in his youthful ignorance, he'd imagined all young women were more like Grace. He'd never imagined one like Lucetta, which is why he hadn't recognized her nature at first. And then it was too late.

Peter climbed back onto the mower and sagged onto the metal seat. He wouldn't trade his daughters for anything. But what a different life it would've been with Grace as his partner.

The Belgians were eager to come in for dinner. Though Peter was hungry, he was less enthused. It was time Grace left. Not just for the nights, but for good from his household. The girls were getting too attached. And him? He'd been too attached for some time. Whether Grace was single or whether she was spoken for, he was not.

It was better for Grace as well. Though she still smiled, it wasn't with the joy she had when she'd arrived. He'd dimmed her glow, just like Lucetta had extinguished his. The knowledge made his stomach twist.

He'd confused her. No surprise, as he felt as if he was hitched to several of his draft horses and they were all pulling in different directions. But one of them had a Bella-like strength, tugging with the knowledge that if he loved her as he did, he had to let her go.

Peter grimaced. He'd see if Lydia was feeling any better since she was further along in her pregnancy and would maybe be able to have the girls at her house again. If not, one of Isaiah Zook's daughters was getting old enough to watch them. She might do it for the pittance he was paying Grace.

He glanced to where Grace was heading down the lane with the girls to get the mail. When she stopped abruptly, Peter frowned, his gaze following hers to see the mailman driving up the lane instead of pausing at the mailbox. The vehicle stopped beside Grace and the girls. Peter's brow furrowed when Grace pointed to where he was unhitching the horses.

He tensed. One of the Belgians swung his head around to see what was taking him so long. Numbly, Peter continued the familiar work while his mind was fixed on the approaching mail carrier.

It had to be something concerning Lucetta.

Peter stared at his dirt-streaked hands as he drew in an extended breath. He would need to fetch her. He would need to wade into whatever tumult Lucetta created for herself and others, and try to set things right. As best as he could, at least.

But things could never be right again.

The confidence he'd been regaining in trickles due to Grace's presence would leave in torrents with the return of Lucetta's sharp and constant criticism. Peter inhaled so sharply he almost set himself to coughing. He could handle it. But what of the girls? They'd been doing so well…

He compressed his lips as their pleas from Monday reverberated through him. Somehow, he would protect them. Even if it meant sending them away from the house. Peter snorted. At least they would then avoid the isolation that Lucetta would bring upon herself with her return, for she would surely be shunned.

Among other things, he couldn't eat at the same table with her. He couldn't take anything from her hand, even a glass of water. If he didn't treat her according to the rules of a *streng Meindung*—a strong shunning—he faced excommunication himself. Ostracized from community events, Lucetta would lose the support system that she desired to return to. And by their association, to some extent, they would be cut off as well. He could handle it. But the girls would be denied the close-knit activities that made their way of life so special. Peter swept a trembling hand down the nearest horse's sweating neck as he waited for the mailman to pull alongside.

Ja. It was best for his daughters if they didn't stay in the house when their mother came back.

And with Lucetta's return, it was definitely time for Grace to leave. Any dreams he'd had regarding her needed to shrivel like corn leaves in a drought.

The mailman rolled down his window. "Fine-looking pair of horses there, Mr. Lehman."

Peter nodded and forced a smile.

"Got a certified letter for you. I'll need you to sign." The man handed a pen and a thick business envelope with a green card on it through the open window. Tucking his elbow hard against his side to control the tremor in his hand, Peter scrawled his signature. The man retrieved his pen, did something with the letter and returned it to Peter's sweating palm.

"Thank you," he murmured, although he was far from thankful.

The mailman tipped his fingers in farewell. "Take care, now." Gravel crunched under his tires as he pulled away. Peter's gaze followed the vehicle as it drove down the lane. He glanced toward the house to see Grace watching him from the porch before he finally stared at the official-looking envelope.

His printed address gave him no clue. Nor did the one in the upper corner, a return address he didn't recognize. The Belgian beside him bobbed its head, jerking the leather lines through Peter's hands. With a sigh, he tucked the letter under his arm and led the team into the barn. Only after he'd tended to them did he retrieve the letter from where he'd wedged it under the top bag of a stack of feed when he'd entered the barn.

His legs felt like lead. He slumped against the stack and frowned at the letter in his hand. The edge of the envelope sliced into his finger as he slit it open. Peter twisted his lips. It wasn't a surprise the paper would cut him, even through his work-calloused hands. Lucetta had cut him in so many ways before. His brows furrowed as he unfolded the pages.

Although there were several pages in Lucetta's scrawling handwriting, the top two sheets were typed. Peter's breath caught as he scanned through them once. He exhaled sharply before reading them again. Only then did he proceed to the handwritten pages behind them.

Carefully returning the papers to the envelope, he braced an elbow on the top feedbag and stared unseeing at his printed name and address. When he lifted his gaze, it immediately met Grace's from where she stood in the open barn door. The feed in the bag shifted under his elbow as he pushed upright.

Trudging like a man three times his age, he crossed to her. At his expression, her eyes widened.

"It's about Lucetta." Peter saw in Grace's countenance that she'd assumed as much. He dragged in a breath. "I need to go. Can you pack some overnight things for the girls and take them to Lydia's?"

Grace's voice was hoarse, but her response was immediate. "I can stay here with them."

Peter almost crumpled in relief. He lifted a heavy hand to rub the back of his neck. "I don't know how long I'll be gone."

"We'll be fine."

"The chores. The hay. The corn still in the wagon." James knew what to do on the chores. Regarding the hay, depending on how long he'd be gone, he could lose most of this cutting. The corn, if it rained on it... Peter sighed. It couldn't be helped. Given the news, who knew what his future on the farm was.

"It will be taken care of."

"I...need to get to the phone shack and contact a driver."

She inhaled sharply through her nose. "I'll make you a sandwich to take."

"Grace…" Her glistening eyes echoed his own. Peter reached out in a helpless gesture. When his hand was clasped by her firm, warm one, he closed his eyes. This was the relationship he'd longed for. A partnership, a friend, a supporter. After a moment, he gave her fingers a gentle squeeze and reluctantly let go.

"I'm not sure when I'll be back." He swallowed hard. "And when I am, I won't be alone."

Chapter Nineteen

Grace jolted, her eyes darting to the window. Was someone coming up the lane? Was it Peter? She took two quick steps to the sink, leaning on the edge of it to look as far as possible down the road when the lane proved empty. Sighing, she sank back onto her heels. Surely it was longer than just yesterday that he'd said he had to leave? Something he'd quickly done after throwing a few items into a suitcase and hugging the girls goodbye.

Sunday night she'd stalked off to her bedroom, so nettled by Peter's actions that she lay awake, listening to the shrill call of the spring peepers long into the night. The repetitious frogs gave her plenty of time to consider those actions, from Peter's unexpected search for a beau to his exasperating behavior that night when one actually arrived.

Peter hadn't wanted another man to court her. Not really. Though in the barn—when he'd spoken her name and clasped her hand—he had shown that he cared. With him now gone to fetch his wife, the knowledge held little comfort.

So why did she long for his return when it would only bring pain in the form of Lucetta?

Grace pressed her hands to her face. *Oh, Grace, you foolish, foolish girl.*

Though she'd not said a word, only answered Malinda and Fannie's questions regarding their father's absence as best she could, somehow the community knew. Jethro Weaver, a distant neighbor, arrived midmorning to rake the hay Peter had cut. Dairy farmer Zebulun Lapp and his sons Josiah, Paul, and Harvey, showed up later that day to empty the wagon of corn back into the silo.

She'd plied them with cookies. Josiah had plied her with smiles and flirtation. Though he'd made her smile at the time, it had faded the moment the Lapp men had gone down the lane. Instead of hearing eligible Josiah's teasing comments, Peter's words resonated through her.

It will never work, Grace.

And when I am, I won't be alone.

Grace bit down on her bottom lip to prevent a sob. *He might not be alone, but I will be.* By the hints Josiah was throwing out, she could walk out with him should she give any encouragement. For sure and certain, he could make her smile and laugh. Was that all it took to make her happy? Would it make her happy for the lifetime they would be together? Why did she feel she'd miss the ache she experienced with Peter? The ache of…being needed. The satisfaction of not only being the recipient of sunshine, albeit it occasionally, but the giver of it. The knowledge of being wanted not just as someone but as…herself.

Peter had made her feel that way. Like she was one piece of a thousand-piece jigsaw puzzle. But it was the only piece that would fit with the surrounding others in his life. His girls, his farm, his wariness, his latent humor. His section of the puzzle might not be the center or most interesting part, but it would have been enough for her.

It will never work, Grace.

And when I am, I won't be alone.

She gave a shuddering exhale. She would leave the house immediately upon his and Lucetta's return. What wife would want another woman in her home? Grace squeezed her eyes shut, blocking out the vision of Peter with his wife. The wife who'd caused those darker parts of Peter. The wife who in all likelihood would contribute to them again.

She couldn't stay and watch. Not in the house. Not in the community? If there was a chance Peter was going to be happy, she could stay. It would hurt, but she could watch him be happy, because even if she wasn't the one to share it with him, just knowing he was happy would give her contentment.

Grace brushed at the tears that trickled from the corner of her eyes. But could she watch him withdraw again? Become so much the season of winter that there was no hint of spring or summer in his nature? That was her fear. Her heartache.

Granted, Lucetta may have changed. After all, *Gott* had changed Saul, a persecutor of Christians, to Paul, an author of many books in the *Biewel*. But if Lucetta hadn't changed... Grace numbly shook her head. She couldn't stay in the community and watch what Lucetta might do to Peter.

And what of the girls? Grace blinked open her eyes and looked out the window to where Malinda and Fannie were making mud pies under the shade of an oak tree. Her hands curled into fists as she recalled their tentative behavior when she'd first arrived. Was she a coward for leaving them? But what could she do when Lucetta was their mother? Peter would protect them as best he could, but he couldn't always be around.

She pursed her lips. At least, before she left, she'd tell Lydia and Miriam of her concerns, though Lydia probably already knew, as Lucetta was her sister.

So, had she decided to leave then? And go where? To another district looking for a teacher? Although they might wonder why she was leaving, the Miller's Creek district would give her a good recommendation.

Or should she go back to Iowa? What with her reluctance to respond and the silo incident, she'd yet to answer her mother's letter. Should she leave Miller's Creek, it would be difficult to explain to her *mamm* why she was moving to another district and not home.

As her heart was already taken, did it really matter who she married? She huffed out a breath. If she moved home, at least someone would be exuberant about a wedding, even though it wouldn't be the bride or the groom. Her *mamm* would be thrilled enough to come up and help her pack.

Not that there would be much to pack. The house had come furnished, the mare and buggy had been provided. All she had were her clothes, some books and... Sunny. Grace pressed her hand against her stomach, which had just dropped the entire depth of the silo. While she, with her books and clothes, could travel to Iowa by bus or hired driver, it was much more costly to transport a pony that distance. Money she didn't have for a pony that her *mamm* would say she didn't need.

She'd have to sell the little mare.

Renewed tears leaked down her cheeks. Grace was too numb to stem them. The sound of a buggy rolling up the lane grew louder before she jerked up the corner of her apron to hastily swipe at tears and make a quick dab at her nose. *Had Peter returned?* Grace hurried outside. When Gideon waved through his open buggy door, she wilted momentarily before squaring her shoulders and striding to meet him as he drew the Standardbred to a halt.

"Looks like I'm a bit late to help out."

"James should be here shortly to do chores, but the others have left for the day. They plan to return tomorrow to put the hay up. If you're available then."

Shifting to sit on the edge of his seat, his blue-clad knees extending through the buggy's doorway, Gideon considered her a moment. "Maybe I'm too late for that. But you look like you could use a little help yourself."

His voice was gentle. Gentle enough to cause more tears to slip down Grace's cheeks. She knuckled them away. "Um, I was wondering. Does your brother Samuel deal in ponies?"

"Samuel deals in anything that neighs or brays and has four legs and a mane and tail. Are you buying or selling?"

Grace sniffed. "S-selling."

Gideon leaned back on the seat to reach for something on the buggy's dash. When he straightened, he handed her a few napkins from the local fast-food joint. "Why?"

Grace took them and mopped at her face. "Bbecause I can't take her with me when I go back to Iowa."

"Why do you need to?"

"Sell her? Because it's too expensive to have her hauled all the way there."

"No. Why do you need to go to Iowa?"

Grace strangled the damp wadded napkins in her hand. "Because it's the reasonable thing to do."

"Reasonable for who?"

"For my *mamm*," Grace blurted. She drew in a long breath. "And for me."

"Why?"

"Because…" Grace looked over her shoulder at the house and the girls. "Because when things change here, I don't think I can stay and watch what happens."

Gideon shrugged a shoulder. "Things are frequently changing. Well, except for our clothes. And transportation. And several other rules we've had for a few hundred years. But circumstances? And people themselves? They change. Are you the same person you were when you moved here?"

"I…" Grace furrowed her brow. Was she? The Grace that moved here wouldn't have bought a pony she didn't need. That Grace would've gone home at her *mamm*'s first letter beckoning her to do so. She sighed. That Grace would've probably had enough sense not to fall in love with a married man.

She shook her head. "No. No, I'm not."

"Then how do you know the same thing is going to happen?" Gideon tipped his head toward the house. "Wouldn't you rather know before you bolt? Does this different person you've become have the courage to stay and find out?"

Did she? The courage to stand firm against her mother's wishes? To stay and see Peter with his wife? And the unhappiness that usually followed in Lucetta's wake? Stay and not be able to do anything about it?

Gideon must've read her face. "Would leaving really hurt any less?"

Grace shook her head again, more slowly this time. She tipped her lips into a half smile. "So, you're saying I shouldn't sell my pony."

He echoed her smile. "Not yet, anyway. And if you do need to, I'll strong-arm my *bruder* into giving you a good price. And make sure the pony gets a good home. And just in case you need more napkins, I'll make sure I keep them on hand."

Once again, Grace had to use the wadded napkins to capture a few tears. "You're a nice man, Gideon Schrock. Why hasn't some girl snapped you up yet?"

His smile stretched into a grin. "What a terrible thing to wish on someone you just called nice."

His expression sobered. "I guess I'm changing too. Maybe I'm working on a little courage myself."

"I hope you find it."

Gideon straightened on the seat and gathered his reins. "Me too. In the meantime, I'll stock napkins enough for the both of us."

Grace waved as he headed down the lane, watching for some time after he turned onto the road. Gideon was right. It would hurt either way. Did she really want to leave Peter and the girls any earlier than she had to?

No.

Grace drew in a long breath. She was going to stay. At least for a little while. Not at the house, but in the community. By her choice. Not because she was trying to please someone or falling into their plans because she had none of her own. She pressed her fingertips to her mouth. It might hurt. It might turn out to be a bad decision. But it was hers. And for the moment, it felt right.

The baby had been crying. Peter tentatively took her into his arms. She immediately nestled her cheek against his chest. Peter drew in a ragged sigh as his arms tightened about her. He held his own breath as her tiny ribs shallowly rose and fell. How could he reject her? There was no considering it. She was his.

"I got here as soon as I could."

"We understand, Mr. Lehman. She couldn't have gone home any earlier as it was. We want to keep her under observation for a bit longer, just to make sure she's out of the woods. In light of her mother's sepsis, we're treating her with antibiotics, just in case. We're glad to see that she's doing so well." The nurse's eyes were compassionate. "I'm sorry about the loss of your wife."

Peter nodded mutely.

"We did all we could for her, but it appeared her prenatal care had been limited. She had an underlying infection and she'd apparently been in labor for a bit before she arrived at the hospital."

He winced, careful to keep his movements from disturbing the baby. "We'd…been apart."

"We gathered that from the letter. She was very insistent that you receive it. She gave us your address."

"Thank you." In Lucetta's letter, she said she'd never really appreciated her community until she left it and wanted to come home. Had she been sincere? Would she have continued to think the same thing if she'd returned? Peter didn't know. Either way, he would've accepted her back. The rest was between her and *Gott*. Some in Peter's community believed in doing the right things to have a relationship with *Gott*. Before he'd left Kentucky, Peter had attended some *Biewel* classes with a friend. They'd taught that *Gott* looks at the heart. That if Lucetta had truly been sincere in her repentance, it was between her and *Gott*. Peter hoped she had been.

Lucetta had named him as father on the child's birth certificate. Peter didn't know the legalities of it. Perhaps, even though he wasn't the child's biological father, she'd had to, as he was her legal husband. He cupped a gentle hand around the babe nestled against his shoulder. It didn't matter. He would raise this little one as his own.

He supposed there'd been an apology of sorts to him in Lucetta's letter. He'd been too numb to decipher it. He was numb now. He felt only regret at her passing. Any relief was tempered by guilt. She had been his wife in the eyes of *Gott*. The mother of children born while they'd been married. How many of their issues had been his fault?

Even though her passing made him free to marry again, what faults would he take into a new relationship? Ones to destroy it as well?

Which was why it still wouldn't work for him and Grace.

Ah, Grace. If I wasn't enough for Lucetta, how could I be enough for you? And if I ask you to stay, you'll think it's only because of what I want you to do, childcare for the infant, as well as Malinda and Fannie. By your own admission, you strive to please people. You'd stay and marry me, even if you didn't want to, just as you'd agreed to marry that Willis fellow.

What do I have to offer you? A struggling farm. I know I'm not all the things Lucetta has taunted me about over the years, but what if there's enough that after a month, a year, two years, you regret marrying me? Peter had to swallow twice to defeat the lump in his throat that threatened to choke him. *You have so many other worthy options. How could I ask you to become mother to three children and wife to a man who couldn't even keep the spouse he had?*

Asking Grace to stay would be the worst thing he could do to her. Though he ached at the thought of doing so when a future for them finally seemed possible, he had to let her go.

So now what? Who would take care of his *kinner* while he worked? With this babe, he certainly couldn't ask Lydia, due to having another little one of her own soon. While the Zook girl could watch Malinda and Fannie, having her take care of a newborn might be something else.

Peter's chest rose and fell on a series of inhalations, almost triggering a cough. He grimaced at the reminder. He could go back to Kentucky, where he had family to help with the girls. His *mamm*. Sisters. Sisters-in-law. It would mean selling the farm. Going back a failure, just as Lucetta had said he was. The *boppeli* in his arms stirred as he tensed. Peter gently rubbed the child's back until she settled down again.

He stared at the far wall of the hospital nursery. He'd need to make arrangements to sell Bella's foal anyway as soon as it was weaned to help cover Lucetta and the child's expenses. Even if they wanted to help, the community she'd chosen to leave shouldn't be responsible for them.

Coldness swept over him like he'd abruptly been dunked into an early spring pond.

What happened to the man he used to be? The one who'd come to Wisconsin with joy and anticipation, eager to build a farm and life in what his uncle had unexpectedly left him. Peter bowed his head. He missed that man. He pressed a soft kiss on the tiny brow tucked against his shoulder. Would that man have been a better father to his expanding family than the man he was now? Probably. His girls deserved joy. All three of his girls.

His lips twitched ruefully. They deserved Grace. But did Grace deserve them? Did he deserve Grace? He lowered his chin until it rested on his chest. Not the man he was now. Not the man he'd become.

Chapter Twenty

"Like this?" Malinda tentatively tucked the bottom of the small shovel under the hen's chest and lifted it. A *ting ting* sounded as the red hen pecked at the coal scoop Grace had found in the basement to use for the task.

"That's right." Grace nodded. "And while you distract her with the shovel, Fannie can reach in and collect the eggs."

Though obviously ready to jerk back at any movement from the hen, Fannie did so. She grinned when she withdrew her hand, a brown egg in her palm.

"Just like that." Grace extended the basket for her to put her prize in and shared the girl's smile.

"Let's do another!"

"All right." Grace's smile slid away at the little one's enthusiasm.

Malinda and Fannie had come far since her arrival. It would be so hard to leave them. Because she cared for them but, more so, for what she feared she'd be leaving them to. Her fingers tightened on the handle of the egg basket. They'd all been working on their courage these past few days. The girls on addressing their fear of the hens and questions regarding their father's absence. He hadn't told them why he was leaving. As for herself, she was bracing herself to stay and witness what Lucetta's return would do to this family she'd grown to love.

Since her conversation with Gideon two days ago, she'd realized that by staying, maybe she *could* help. The girls would be in school at some point, and if she stayed single, as a schoolteacher, she could support them. Encourage their confidence. It wouldn't help Peter, not directly, but perhaps it would in some small way benefit him, knowing the girls were being helped.

There'd still been no word from him. Neither to her nor to any of the men who'd come yesterday to put up the hay. Grace was growing worried. Had Peter left for the *Englisch* world as well? Her stomach twisted. Had Lucetta persuaded him to jump the fence with her? Even as the thought popped in—again—Grace shook her head vehemently. Lucetta might leave her children, but Peter never would. Though he might doubt himself, she didn't. He was a *gut* man. And he'd never do anything to hurt his girls.

A muted clatter jerked her out of her musings. Grace looked over to see the small shovel rolling across the straw strewn floor as Malinda, with Fannie a step behind her, disappeared out the coop door.

"Girls?" Had they been pecked? Had their newfound courage already evaporated?

Then she heard it. The sound of a vehicle driving up the lane. Not a buggy but a motorized one. Like the one Peter had hired when he'd left. Clutching the egg basket in front of her like a shield, Grace ducked out the low door and looked beyond the running girls to where an older van was stopping in front of the house.

He was back. Her heart raced with excitement before thudding heavily with apprehension as she corrected herself. *They* were back.

Only when she noticed the eggs clacking against each other did Grace realize she was trembling. Her attention fixed on the van, she slowly crossed the chicken run to the gate—flung wide in the girls' hasty departure—and closed it behind her. Fearing in her anxious state she might break an egg or two, or the whole basketful, she carefully set it down.

Her breath hitched when the door slid open and Peter stepped out. He immediately squatted to take the girls into his arms. All Grace could see of him over their heads was his gaze, which had landed, and remained, on her. Even across the distance, she read fatigue and worry in it. And something else as well?

Finally, he bent his head toward the girls. After a moment of apparent discussion, with them still in his arms, he rose to his feet and turned toward the interior of the van. Grace exhaled and twisted her hands together, waiting for Lucetta's appearance. When a minute passed and no one exited the vehicle other than the gray-haired driver, who opened the back of the van to extract an old suitcase and other assorted bags, which he then carried up to the porch, her brow furrowed.

Peter set the girls down and closed the sliding door. Malinda and Fannie skipped after him as he passed behind the van to open the sliding door on its far side. After an endless moment, that door slid shut, along with the driver's door. The vehicle's motor started. It pulled away, circling the barnyard to head back down the lane.

Grace stayed frozen by the chicken run. There were only three left standing in front of the house: Peter, Malinda and Fannie. The girls came running toward her. Upon reaching her, they each grabbed one of her hands.

"Come see our baby sister!"

"Your baby..." Grace could barely form the words. She could see now that Peter cradled something in one arm. A *boppeli*? Where had it come from? Where was Lucetta? Grace had to move her feet to keep up with the girls' tugs. Her gaze again met Peter's. And held.

"Where's…" her voice trailed off.

He grimaced before glancing at the baby in his arms. "Maternal sepsis. I'm sorry. I should have told you before I left. I should have called. But I didn't want to leave a message at the phone shack. I was just…stunned and…" Peter lowered his head. "Embarrassed." His shoulders rose and fell on a heavy sigh. "What kind of man am I that my wife would run off with another man and have his child?"

Gently releasing the girls' hands, Grace clasped Peter's free one where it dangled at his side. "A *gut* man. A faithful man. A man who will be a *wunderbar daed* to that child." She glanced to where Malinda and Fannie, having deserted them, were looking through the bags the *Englisch* driver had left by the door. "And has been a *wunderbar* one to others."

Her thoughts were scattered more than dandelion fluff in an erratic wind at the changed circumstances. Grace tried to gather them in. Slowly collecting them, and reassured by the gentle squeeze of his fingers, she searched for words, and her courage.

"A man I would be happy to have as *daed* to my own children. And as…a husband." Grace rolled her lips inward, biting them. Had she said too much? Too much, too soon?

"Grace," Peter lifted their entwined hands to

his mouth and gently kissed the back of one of hers. "I wasn't enough for Lucetta. I don't know that I can be the man you need. I've already failed at being a husband."

"Peter, you weren't the failure. As much as I hurt for you in believing that, I would be grateful for the chance to share my life with you and show you how *wunderbar* of a man you truly are."

She almost wept at the hope in his eyes before it dimmed and he shook his head.

"By your own words, Grace, you want to please people. You'd fall in with me just to help. I couldn't ask it of you, because I lo—" He winced. "*Ach*, just because…"

"You weren't. You aren't." She grinned. "I think I just asked you. Don't leave me twice embarrassed by wrongly assuming a man was interested in marrying me." Her expression sobered. "I couldn't bear it if it wasn't true with you."

Peter hissed in a breath as he studied her expression. He gestured with their entwined hands to the farmyard. "You think you can bear this?"

"With joy." She arched her eyebrows at him. "And Peter? I'm not Lucetta."

A corner of his mouth lifted in a half smile. "That, I know."

"Even though you scoured the district looking for others for me, the man I need is you." She released his hand to loop an arm around his lean waist. "*Gut* thing, as you're also the man I love."

Peter closed his eyes. A shudder swept through him.

As running footfalls announced Malinda and Fannie's rapid approach, Peter's eyes popped open again. The girls stood on tiptoe to peer at the baby.

"When is she going to wake up? And what's her name, *Daed*?"

"*Ja, Daed.* What's her name?" Fannie echoed.

Peter looked down at the *boppeli* cuddled in his arm. "I... She doesn't have one yet."

"She has to have a name. Can we name her? We're practiced at picking them out."

"You certainly are, Fannie." Peter paused. After a moment, he brushed a gentle finger down the baby's cheek. "But I have one in mind for her. A *gut* one, I think." He slipped his free arm around Grace and nestled her against his side. To Grace, it felt like sliding into place. A perfect fit.

"We're going to name her for something I never envisioned having in my life again. Something that came back, because of Grace."

"What is it?" Fannie was bouncing up and down in her excitement.

Peter's gaze met Grace's. She drew in a breath at the happiness that shone from it.

"Hope. Her name is Hope."

Epilogue

"Am I doing it right?"

"*Ja*, Fannie. Start at the neck and work your way back." Grace, holding one-month-old Hope, coached from outside Sunny's stall.

Fannie ran the brush over one side of the golden pony while her sister worked from the other. "When I'm bigger than Malinda, will I be old enough to groom Tanner?"

"By that time, Tanner will be a lot bigger as well. Maybe even bigger than Bella."

"Tanner is going to be a *daadi* horse. Isn't that right, *Daed*?"

Peter looked over from where he was graining the draft horses along the opposite wall. "*Ja*. When he's old enough." Though he smiled, he rubbed a hand across the back of his neck.

Grace knew the support of the community since he'd come home with Hope still embarrassed and humbled him. When he'd told Samuel Schrock he needed to sell Tanner to help cover hospital costs, Samuel had suggested, instead of selling, to make arrangements with others to breed their draft mares with the colt when he matured. Paying him now for foals later. So the contributions felt less like charity and more like Peter was earning them. The rest of the hospital costs, much to Peter's humble appreciation, came from the church community fund by unanimous consent.

Grace gently patted the baby's back as she watched Peter work. Hope had indeed made an impact on their household. It was taking encouragement, but day by day, Peter was finding confidence in himself. And in them as a couple.

The knowledge that his asthma wouldn't force him from the farm had helped. Though he still occasionally coughed in the barn—something helped with use of an inhaler and other breathing exercises he'd since learned after reluctantly returning to the doctor—it had been determined the biggest irritant was corn dust. Other farmers in the district were working with him, trading labor for grain among other things, to help limit his exposure and keep him farming.

Grace smiled when Peter crossed the barn to lean on the stall's half wall and supervise the brushing with her.

"I heard back from my *mamm*. Though she's not thrilled that we're getting married here instead of in Iowa, my family is coming up for the wedding. And I finally told Isaiah Zook I wouldn't be teaching this fall." She sighed. "I should've told him earlier."

"I'm sure he already knew and was just giving you time before you needed to move out of the rental house. As president of the school board, he's probably already been searching for a teacher for the fall." With a quick glance to ensure Malinda and Fannie were occupied with their grooming, Peter leaned over to kiss Grace. "Since you can't as you'll soon be a married woman."

At the sound of giggling, they jerked back to find Malinda and Fannie watching them from the stall's interior. Grace's cheeks heated. Being able to share her affection with Peter was still so new. And so precious. She bit back a smile when Peter blushed as well.

"It's all right, *Daed*," Malinda assured them. "You can kiss her. It makes us happy." She and Fannie covered their mouths and tittered behind their fingers.

Peter glanced at Grace. She loved seeing the joyful glint that shone in them. "What do you think? You're the one who likes to please people."

"I think it's a fine idea. One I'll come up with myself. Frequently." With the babe tucked in her arms and the sound of the girls giggling a short distance away, Grace lifted her face for another, more lingering kiss.

"I think," Peter murmured against her lips, "when Lydia's *boppeli* is born, we should do something very nice for it. Without its pending arrival and Miriam's suggestion, you—" he leaned his forehead against hers "—and this renewed feeling of …hope, might never have come to this household."

"Lydia was never that ill or tired," Grace confessed in a whisper.

"Really? I guess I owe the three of you then." Peter gently wagged his head. "I never figured watching a woman fall asleep in church would give me more than I could ever imagine."

* * * * *

Dear Reader,

I can't believe this is my tenth book in the Miller's Creek series! I never imagined when I typed the opening lines of Ruth's story, *The Amish Bachelor's Choice*, in 2017, that I would have the opportunity to write ten stories. And it's thanks to you, dear reader. I have learned many things in those years. Things about the Amish, about what kinds of birds, insects, even snakes might be located in a certain area of Wisconsin, about all sorts of factors that might affect the characters in a story, from RSV to grain silos, to information about the restaurant business. That's not even including everything I've learned about writing, and about social media!

But the best thing I've learned is how wonderful and supportive the Love Inspired readers are. Thanks so much for your support and for letting me into your world.

All the best,
Jocelyn McClay

Harlequin® Reader Service

Enjoyed your book?

Try the perfect subscription for Romance readers and get more great books like this delivered right to your door.

See why over 10+ million readers have tried Harlequin Reader Service.

Start with a Free Welcome Collection with free books and a gift—valued over $20.

Choose any series in print or ebook. See website for details and order today:

TryReaderService.com/subscriptions